SAY YOU LOVE ME

The misery in his voice tore at her heart as a knot enlarged in her throat. She turned and his lips landed hard against hers in a deep demanding kiss. His dark, rich taste seeped into her mouth, into her blood, causing it to burn. When he caught her lower lip between his teeth, her resultant shudder sent thousands of tingling sensations throughout her body. Her head filled with the sounds of a roaring hurricane, and her body burned as bright as the sun itself.

Jordan ran his hands along her smooth curves and taut muscles with a suave, practiced touch that quickened her breath and solicited a murmur of pleasure.

He pulled her closer and dragged his mouth down to her throat.

Caught up in their private world, small bits of reality pried its way into Christian's blurry thoughts. She gingerly opened her eyes. It took all of her strength to pull away.

"This isn't right," she managed to gasp.

"Of course it is. We're married."

BOOK YOUR PLACE ON OUR WEBSITE AND MAKE THE ARABESQUE ROMANCE CONNECTION!

We've created a customized website just for our very special Arabesque readers, where you can get the inside scoop on everything that's going on with Arabesque romance novels.

When you come online, you'll have the exciting opportunity to:

- View covers of upcoming books

- Learn about our future publishing schedule (listed by publication month and author)

- Find out when your favorite authors will be visiting a city near you

- Search for and order backlist books

- Check out author bios and background information

- Send e-mail to your favorite authors

- Join us in weekly chats with authors, readers and other guests

- Get writing guidelines

- AND MUCH MORE!

Visit our website at
http://www.arabesquebooks.com

SAY YOU LOVE ME

Adrianne Byrd

ARABESQUE
★BET
BOOKS

BET Publications, LLC
www.msbet.com
www.arabesquebooks.com

ARABESQUE BOOKS are published by

BET Publications, LLC
c/o BET BOOKS
One BET Plaza
1900 W Place NE
Washington, D.C. 20018-1211

First Printing: January, 2000

10 9 8 7 6 5 4 3 2 1

Printed in the United States of America

For Channon and Charla.
Aim for the stars.

The night has a thousand eyes,
And the day but one,
Yet the light of the whole bright world dies
With the dying sun

The mind has a thousand eyes,
And the heart but one,
Yet the light of a whole life dies
When love is done

—*Francis William Bourdillion*

One

"I want a divorce."

Silence cloaked the room as Christian Williams's guilt-ridden words hung in the air while her gaze remained locked on her half-eaten dinner. The soft shuffling of the servant's feet and then the soft click of the sliding door signaled they'd left her alone to deal with a man she didn't know anymore—her husband.

The tension thickened and robbed her of the confidence she'd spent months building. *Look at him,* her inner voice commanded. That simple task proved to be the hardest thing she'd ever done. With balled fists and a shaky disposition, Christian forced her gaze to meet Jordan's.

The eight-foot glass dinner table might as well have been a mile long—a good symbol of the distance that had grown between them.

Jordan's midnight-colored eyes clouded from a brewing storm. Her heart nearly stopped, and in its place a sharp, unbearable pain pulsed with every breath she took. Evidence of her husband's Spanish-American heritage dominated his strong features. With short-cropped, wavy hair and eyes darker than the darkest night, his distinguished, sophisticated looks never failed to turn heads.

Christian's gaze caressed his skin's golden hue with longing. She turned away when she realized what she was doing. However, her courage restored, she chanced another look. This time, she focused on the subtle signs of maturity that graced his eyes, then his salt-and-pepper mustache, which added to his masculinity.

The soft lighting from the chandelier illuminated the room. Tiny lines along his jaw twitched, a sure sign of his anger.

She waited, waited for an inevitable explosion.

He lowered his fork, then wiped the corners of his mouth, all the while never breaking eye contact.

Why doesn't he say something? Anything would be better than this silence. The silence condemned her, accused her of a terrible crime.

"I'm sorry," she said. Her tears struggled for release. Pain flickered across her husband's hardened expression, then disappeared. Was she wrong about his feelings? She couldn't be sure, not until he said something. Anything.

Seconds stretched into minutes, confirming her worst fears. He didn't care. J.W. Enterprises was the only thing that mattered. The company he'd started years ago had practically become the air he breathed, and she refused to compete with it any longer for his time, or his love.

Against her will, tears brimmed and blurred

her vision, but she refused to let them fall. Her chair screeched like a locomotive as she stood from the table. With as much dignity as she could muster, she pulled the four carat diamond ring from her finger and placed it on the table, along with its matching gold band.

It's over, her head shouted, but her heart begged to stay. In that same instant, Jordan broke eye contact to stare at the golden rings.

Christian turned and forced one foot in front of the other. In truth, she wanted him to stop her, to ask her to reconsider, but it didn't happen. The clicking of her heels against the marble floor echoed in her ears. He wasn't coming after her. The realization threatened to choke her. Weak-kneed, she managed to make it out of the dining room, relieved that he couldn't see the tears that finally streamed down her face.

Don't go. Jordan exhaled. Denial took hold of his heart as he waited in vain for his wife to return. He would not, could not, believe what had just happened. *A divorce?* His gaze returned to the two rings. A deep ache penetrated and settled within him.

Snatching his wineglass, he emptied its contents in one gulp. He closed his eyes, and with a trembling hand lowered his glass. *What could be wrong?* He looked around at the exquisite furnishings, at the rewards he'd been able to provide. He'd made sure Christian had the best of everything. Never had he denied her anything.

Sure, they had their share of problems, but they always managed to work things out. Here lately, his company demanded most of his time, forcing him to travel five to six days out of the week, but Christian understood all of that—didn't she?

Jordan stood, tossing down the white linen napkin from his lap. His gaze returned to the rings. Fear gripped him, while the image of his wife removing her jewels replayed in his mind.

Neglect. That was it. He hadn't spent as much time with her as he'd like to, but the situation was just temporary. With his company's new software hitting the market in the coming months, he'd been subjected to a tremendous amount of pressure.

Too much time had passed. It was now or never. He needed to talk to her. The pain mirrored in Christian's expression haunted him. Her brimming tears broke his heart.

He went to the end of the table and retrieved her rings. He squeezed them in his hand, then left the dining room to confront his wife. As he walked up the massive mahogany staircase, apprehension jumbled the words in his head. Two servants skittered out of his path when he reached the top level, but he hardly noticed. He needed a plan.

First, he'd apologize, for whatever he was guilty of. Then he'd promise to spend more time with her. That should make her happy. And when she forgave him—*if* she forgave him—he'd shower her with roses, jewelry, whatever it took.

At the bedroom door, he drew a deep breath and opened his fist. The two golden rings glittered back at him.

Jordan pushed open the door and stepped inside.

Something was wrong. At first glance, the room's picturesque decor looked normal. However, the anxiety trickling through his veins warned him otherwise. Something was definitely wrong.

He moved in farther and took a closer look. Where was she? Fear returned as he rushed toward the walk-in closet. As he passed Christian's vanity, sparse items littered the glass top. As he threw open the closed door, time stopped. Rows of naked hangers hung from the rods.

Jordan retreated and refused to believe his eyes. She wasn't gone. Making a one hundred and eighty degree turn, he sprinted toward the bathroom. More of her things were gone.

The weight of the rings drew his attention. He opened his hand and stared at them again. He could no longer deny the truth. *She left me.* Numb, he returned to the master bedroom in a daze.

When he plopped onto the bed, something crinkled beneath him. Shifting his weight, he pulled out some papers. Delta tickets? *Where is she going?* He flipped the envelope open and stared at the two tickets. Destination: Bermuda. More questions formed in his head. Departure: September 18. That was yesterday. He rummaged through the other papers and found hotel reservations for a honeymoon suite.

Jordan looked again at the word *honeymoon*. September 18. *Their wedding anniversary.* He'd forgotten their anniversary . . . again.

Damn.

Two

For two hours Christian drove around the city of Atlanta, listening to the steady rhythm of the windshield wipers blend with the music on the radio. Its mournful tunes about lost love intensified her misery and elevated her loneliness. The night's events seemed too surreal, too inconceivable.

She exited off I 285 and drove to Courtlane Highrises in the heart of downtown. Once inside the parking deck she cut the car's engine, then slumped back in her seat and let silence encase her. Her fragile emotions swirled inside her, bringing her, at times, to the brink of hopelessness.

She couldn't convince herself that this was for the best, or that she was doing the right thing. If any of that was true, then why did she hurt so much? Why did she feel as if her world, and her life, were over?

A car alarm squealed out a warning in the distance, jerking her from her reverie. She took a cautious look around, then stepped out of the car.

In the lobby, a young man asked if she needed help with her bags, but Christian refused the offer and handled the task alone. When she reached the door with a plastic smile in place, she hesitated.

She wasn't ready for this. The last thing she wanted or needed was sympathy, especially from her best friend, Alexandria.

Christian shook her head at the lie. If she didn't want or need any of that, then why was she there?

She knocked.

Her heartbeat quickened as she prepared for the onslaught of questions. After a few seconds, she feared Alex might be asleep. Glancing down at her luggage, she contemplated whether she should find a hotel for the night.

A series of locks clicked and turned, pulling Christian's attention back toward the door.

When it yanked open, Alex's almond-shaped eyes widened in alarm. "I don't believe it. You left him?"

Christian walked past her six-foot friend to enter the apartment. The entryway, shaped like a luminous glass capsule paved in limestone, gave the apartment a unique look. "I like your new place," she commented.

"Don't change the subject. What happened?" Alex gestured to the luggage outside her door. "And what's all this?"

"Almost everything I own." Christian's tears threatened to return, but she blinked her eyes dry, then got busy grabbing bags.

Alex said nothing as she turned and helped her best friend place the suitcases in the guest bedroom.

When they were done, they went into the living room.

Christian plopped down onto the white, kidney-shaped couch and leaned back to stare up at the curved ceiling.

"I'll fix us a pot of coffee," Alex offered, disappearing into the kitchen.

"What have I done?" Christian whispered. She closed her eyes and prayed for strength and guidance.

Soon, the fresh scent of coffee drifted from the kitchen, filling the entire apartment with its wonderful aroma.

Alex returned and turned on the stereo. The soft, soothing voice of Nancy Wilson played through the speakers.

"Do you *want* to talk about it?" Alex joined Christian on the couch.

"I don't know where to begin." Her defenses weakened under Alex's concerned scrutiny. "I just know it's over." Her voice cracked and her lips trembled, but no tears fell.

"I'm sorry."

"Not as sorry as I am." Christian laughed cynically.

"Don't do this to yourself."

She clasped her hands together and studied her braided fingers. "I just wish I knew where we went wrong. I know J.W. Enterprises plays a big part in it, but where did we go wrong as a couple?"

"What did Jordan say?"

She shook her head. "That's just it, he didn't say anything. He just sat there."

"He wasn't hurt or angry?"

Christian stood from the couch. "I don't know. He didn't respond. I made this huge announcement, and he could care less."

"Jordan loves you."

With her arms crossed, Christian paced the floor, then reached a decision. "I'm not ready for this right now. Can I skip the coffee? I just want to go to bed."

Alex walked to the floor-to-ceiling windows and slid the panels of white silk over to block the night's cityscape. "I'm leaving tomorrow afternoon to go to a fashion show in California. Do you want to talk over breakfast?"

"That will be nice."

Their gazes locked, then the women embraced.

Christian drew what strength she could from her friend before pulling away. "I'll see you in the morning."

Moments later, she dropped onto the bed in the guest room and removed her pumps. She rubbed her aching feet and thought about taking a soothing bubble bath. When she stood again, she walked across the carpet to stand behind the folding screens, which were shaped to resemble architectural columns.

She unfastened the pearl-shaped buttons on her ivory pants suit and refused to allow her troubled thoughts to return to her marriage.

She entered the white marble bathroom and ran her bathwater. Borrowing some of Alex's scented oil beads, she poured more than a generous amount into the steaming water. She pulled towels from the cabinet beneath the bathroom sink and placed them along the expanded ledge surrounding the tub. When she stripped out of the last of her underwear, she stopped in front of the mirror.

Funny, no matter how many times she saw her reflection she never quite got used to her altered body. When she was just twenty years old, doctors had diagnosed her with an advanced stage of breast cancer. Within a week, she had undergone a mastectomy. Years later, she was still trying to come to terms with it, despite the implants.

Christian stepped into the tub while her favorite scent of jasmine filled the bathroom. The hot water relaxed her weary body. Reaching for the soap, she closed her eyes. An instant image of Jordan appeared in her mind.

Leisurely, she lathered her body while dreaming about being in her husband's arms, hearing his rich laughter, and loving him with all her heart.

Then she opened her eyes and stared at her naked fingers. A sense of emptiness engulfed her.

Was there someone else? That thought almost destroyed her. Was J.W. Enterprises solely responsible for the change in Jordan? She didn't know anymore. She only knew that she'd suffered weeks of loneliness, while he spent his nights at his company. Broken promises, broken engagements, the list went on and on. Even now, she didn't doubt that her husband hadn't realized that he'd forgotten their wedding anniversary.

Of course, when he did remember he would have showered her with gifts, flowers, everything he thought she wanted—everything—but himself.

By the time Christian stepped out of the tub, the bubbles had long disappeared. She grabbed a towel and dried off. After a few trips to her bags, she removed her makeup and slipped her favorite robe on. She turned off the bathroom light, then strolled into the bedroom.

She stopped and glanced out the window. She ignored the city below and stared up at the stars. What was Jordan doing? What was he thinking? When a shooting star streaked across the skyline, she closed her eyes and made a wish.

Jordan opened his eyes. It was a silly wish. He turned and entered the bedroom from the veranda. He stumbled as he made it back to his bottle of Jack Daniels. His gaze traveled to the silver frame setting on the bed's end table. He picked up the picture and stared at Christian and her grandmother Bobby.

The striking similarity between the two women never ceased to amaze him. Christian's hair had grown longer since the first time they'd met. It now rested on her shoulders. Both women shared the same breath-taking smile, as well as their dark, soulful eyes.

Jordan fell across the bed, and with his free hand poured another drink. He drained his glass in one gulp, then waited for the alcohol to numb the pain in his heart, but it never happened.

In the hours since Christian had left, he'd ridden a roller coaster of wild emotions. He went from being angry, first with himself then with her, to fear and hopelessness.

"She'll be back," he vowed with confidence, then placed his glass on the table. He had to believe that. No way would he accept that she'd walk out of his life. In the back of his mind, a voice whispered, *if your own father could, what would make your wife any different?*

Lying back against the pillows, he allowed the memory of their first meeting, years ago, to play. . . .

"You're late," Rosa Chavez Williams scolded her son as he entered the house.

"I know, Mama." Jordan closed the heavy, mahogany door behind him. Music and laughter drifted throughout the house and pulled his attention away from his mother. He looked past her to see men and women dressed in formal attire. "Is Malcolm home, yet?" He headed up the stairs.

"Of course he's here. Everyone's here. Dinner was served almost two hours ago," she chastised, following him.

He entered his old bedroom and smiled at the tuxedo draped across the bed.

"I knew you'd be late." Rosa patted his shoulder, then encouraged him to hurry.

Jordan turned and kissed his mother. "I'll be down in twenty minutes. By the way, what's the big occasion?"

"Your brother has some secret announcement he wants to make to the family. I hope it's not what I think it is," she said with a tinge of fear laced in her voice.

"What's that?" He stripped out of his shirt.

"That he wants to marry that dreadful girl." Rosa's hands covered her heart as if the possibility would kill her.

"What girl?" His gaze focused on her.

"Never you mind. If you came and visited more often you'd know what's going on with your own family. Now hurry up." She turned and closed the door behind her.

Jordan rushed into the adjoining bathroom. After years of family protocol, and despite how much he hated these elaborate parties, he was used to dressing in record time.

Tonight's party gave him a reprieve from his

own announcement to the family. He was grateful.

Twenty minutes later, he'd dressed and descended the stairs to join the family. He winced at seeing his father, Noah, leaning against the bottom post.

"Hiding?" Jordan asked.

"I hate formal functions," Noah mumbled. "I think your mother invited half of Georgia here tonight."

"We have that many people?"

Noah nodded.

"What's the occasion? Everybody has kept me in the dark."

"Your brother wants to make some kind of announcement. I know it had better be good for the tab your mother ran up."

Jordan held a hand across his stomach as he laughed at his father's penny-pinching ways. "Since I've missed dinner, maybe we can get someone to fix us a couple of sandwiches."

Noah's eyes twinkled. "Good idea."

Slapping his father's back, Jordan continued in good humor, "Mom isn't going to like our skipping out on the party."

Noah wrinkled his nose. "She's got to find us first."

The kitchen was a madhouse as servants dashed in and out with various hors d'oeuvres for the party.

Head in the refrigerator, Jordan searched for something to make a decent sandwich.

Noah grumbled as he watched the servants. "This is insane."

This was the perfect time, Jordan encouraged himself. Yet, he still didn't know how to tell his father the news that would undoubtedly break his heart.

Noah broke into his son's reverie. "I'm glad you were able to make it."

Jordan smiled as he placed condiments on the counter. Try as he might, he couldn't get the right words organized in his head.

His father reached over and made his own sandwich.

"How's the development of the North Carolina location coming along?"

"Fine, just fine."

"Your mother wants to throw you a party next month. She says that it's not every day one of our sons manages his own office, or something like that. I think she's just looking for an excuse to throw another party."

"That's not necessary."

"I know, but your mother gets excited when it comes to planning these things. I, on the other hand, break out in a cold sweat." Noah held Jordan's gaze as he added, "I wish I could get your brother interested in school, but he's as bad as your mother—spend, spend, spend. It's a wonder we're not living in the streets."

Jordan laughed. "To hear you tell it, you'd think the company was near bankruptcy."

"Ha! My competitors would love that."

Jordan frowned at the dark shadow that crossed his father's features, but it quickly vanished.

"The fact is, Opulence is a solid business," Noah declared. "We've made record sales for the third quarter in a row. I have plans for this next quarter. Big plans."

A piece of Jordan's sandwich wedged in his dry throat. *I have to tell him.*

"I was thinking," his father continued. "What do you think about opening another store in the Gwinnett Mall area?"

Grimacing, Jordan swallowed. "I think I need something to wash this down." He avoided the subject by turning to retrieved two glasses and a gallon of milk from the refrigerator.

Noah's tight scrutiny followed him. "You didn't answer me," he pressed.

Jordan filled their glasses, then locked gazes with his father. "I think that's a good idea." *Tell him.*

They ate in silence while Jordan figured out a way to make his announcement. What was he so afraid of? Hadn't his father always been supportive?

"I need to talk to you about something, Pop."

"I figured as much."

"You did?"

"I don't have to be a rocket scientist to know something is on your mind."

Here goes. "I wanted to talk to you about the business. I know how much you want me in the

North Carolina office, but I've been thinking."
Jordan took another gulp of milk. His stomach
twisted into knots with each word he spoke. "You
know how much I've always wanted to pursue a
career in computers, and I think that now is perfect time for me to branch off and do that." It
didn't quite come out the way he'd hoped, but
at least he'd made the announcement.

Noah's mocha skin color reddened. "Computers?"

Jordan flinched. *Here it comes.* He watch his father's eyes darken.

"Why all of a sudden do you want to play on
computers?"

Jordan exhaled. This wasn't going well. "I
don't want to play on computers. I want to make
computers easier, better. The world of technology
fascinates me. I want to start my own company
and—"

"Start your own company?" Noah backed away
from the counter as if Jordan's words had
burned him.

"I know you think this is crazy, but hear me
out."

"You're not saying anything I want to hear.
What am I supposed to do now? I've worked
hard for this family, and what do I get? Nothing!"

Jordan averted his gaze as guilt engulfed him.

His father raged on, "I have one son that treats
me like the First National Bank and another that
wants to walk out on me."

"It's nothing like that, Pop. I've been thinking about this for a while, and I really want to do this. I'd expected your support in this decision."

Noah's jaw twitched. "You'll be back." He waved his finger. "This crazy computer idea of yours will fail, and you'll be back." He pivoted and stormed out of the kitchen.

Jordan closed his eyes and fought the wave of disappointment that washed over him.

A roar of applause thundered through the house. He guessed his brother had made his announcement. Jordan hated that he had missed it, but he lacked the strength to mingle with a crowd tonight.

"Are you all right, sir?" Clarence, the family butler and good friend, asked from the kitchen door.

"Yeah, I think so. Pop is just upset."

"Yes, sir, I noticed that. Will *you* be all right?"

Jordan shook his head. "I need some fresh air. If anyone needs me, tell them I'll be out in the gardens."

Sympathy pooled in the older man's eyes. "Yes, sir."

Christian McKinley wiped at her tears. Tonight had been a complete disaster. She looked down at the five carat diamond ring that glittered on her finger. How had she gotten herself into this mess?

Her best friend, Alexandria, walked up behind her in the garden. "Chris, are you all right?"

Trying to put on a brave face, Christian smiled, but shook her head in contradiction. "Alex, this is too much. I can't marry him. I can't marry anyone." Alex said nothing as she grasped Christian's hand to offer support.

"I didn't even know he felt this way toward me." Christian glanced up at her six-foot friend and caught the vacant look in her expression. "Hello?" She waved a hand in front of her friend's face. "Are you there?"

"Oh, I'm sorry." Alex blinked, and smiled apologetically. "What were you saying?"

"I was just saying how much of a shock all this is. Are you sure you're okay?"

"Yeah, I'm fine. Look, girl, he's the one who put you on the spot. He shouldn't have proposed to you in front of all those people. You had already told him you weren't looking for a serious relationship."

"I couldn't turn him down in front of his family and friends," Christian rationalized to Alex, as well as to herself. "But I shouldn't have given him false hope by accepting this ring, either."

Alex looked toward the house and exhaled a long sigh. She turned her gaze to Christian and in a low voice asked, "Do you love him?"

"Of course I love him." She hesitated before continuing. "But more like a brother. I mean, he's one of my dearest friends. I had no idea that he felt this way about me." She stared back down at the ring.

"Then there's no way around it. You're going to have to talk to him," Alex said in a shaky whisper as she folded her arms protectively in front of her.

The uncharacteristic action didn't go unnoticed by Christian. "Are you sure you're okay?"

"Yeah, I'm fine." Alex uncrossed her arms. "I think I'm as shocked as you are."

Shaking her head, Christian fought desperately to make sense of the situation. "You're good friends with Malcolm. Has he ever said anything to you about me . . . about this?" She made a wide sweep with her hands.

"Do you want me to go find him for you?"

Christian closed her eyes. She didn't want to hurt Malcolm's feelings. She knew that after this night their relationship would change forever. Inhaling to gather her courage, she nodded. Her friend was right. The sooner she got this over with, the better.

"If you want, afterward, I can take you back to the dorm."

"Thanks, Alex." Christian leaned over and hugged her friend. "Thanks for everything."

"It's no problem. I'll go and get Malcolm."

Jordan strolled along the stone garden walkway, still angry at how everything had blown up in his face. He couldn't blame his father for turning his back on him. The family had expected him to take over Opulence one day. Their once small jewelry store had now turned into a huge conglomerate. Malcolm had made it clear that he wanted no part of the family business, so they all expected Jordan to do the right thing.

He inhaled the fresh fragrances from the garden's various flowers. The leisurely walk had always calmed him in the past, and he sought the same refuge this evening. His father's dismissive and cold attitude toward Jordan's future plans hurt him, but it only made him more determined to prove that he wouldn't fail in his endeavor.

As he rounded a small bend, he found his usual hiding place occupied by a beautiful intruder.

She wore a short, glimmering, white sequined dress with thin straps; in her hands, she held a matching purse. She heard his footsteps and turned to face him. Her beautiful dark chocolate complexion brought to mind a true African Queen.

He moved closer, unable to trust his eyes.

"You scared me," she said, then looked away.

Jordan smiled, unable to believe his luck.

"I'm glad you came out here," she rushed on. "I wanted to talk to you in private."

Curious, Jordan crossed his arms. "Really?" Had he met this beauty before? Surely, he hadn't. How could he ever have forgotten meeting her? He could tell she was nervous about something from the way she kept twirling the strap of her handbag around her fingers and avoiding his gaze. "Is something wrong?"

A weak smile lifted the corners of her lips. "I don't know what to make of all this." She struggled with her words. She blushed prettily and continued, "When I came here tonight, I had no idea that . . ." Her sentence died as she shook her head.

"Are you uncomfortable?" Jordan asked, puzzled.

Her expression sobered. "I'm out of place." She played with the strap again. "I didn't know why you brought me here tonight, Malcolm."

"Oh." He understood now, "I'm not . . ."

"Please, let me finish. I know we became fast friends, and I've enjoyed the six months that we've been seeing each other, but the fact is, I consider you more like a brother. And I want us to remain good friends. I didn't expect you to propose to me in front of all those people."

"But you don't understand—"

She gave him a pleading look that silenced him. Jordan shifted his weight. Her sad expression wrenched his heart.

"All of this is just too grand for me. Hell, I borrowed this dress from Alex." Her attempt at humor failed. "Please try to understand." She pulled the ring from her finger. "I can't accept this."

He lowered his gaze, and his heart tightened as he accepted the ring. *An engagement ring?*

"I'd better go now." She turned.

"Wait!"

She faced him, a sad smile in place. "Malcolm, you know this makes sense. There is still so much you don't know about me, about my family. I accepted the ring because I couldn't . . . I would never embarrass you in front of your family and friends. I just hope that we can still be friends."

Jordan's gut wretched at the sight of her turning away from him, her head held high. He had a sudden premonition that he would never see her again. He panicked. "Can I at least—"

She stopped and faced him.

"Can I at least kiss you good-bye?" *What made me ask that?* The moment he looked back into her earthy brown eyes, a hunger ebbed at his heart. He wanted her.

She smiled nervously, then moved closer to grant him his request.

Jordan leaned down and tilted her chin up with his fingers. The kiss was meant to be a light peck, but as a fire ignited within him it deepened into something powerful. It thrilled him to feel her body arched against his. Her erotic jasmine scent seduced his senses, and before he knew it he had enclosed her in his embrace.

"What in the hell is going on?" A familiar voice thundered.

Jumping apart, they turned to stare at Jordan's twin brother, Malcolm.

Three

Back at Alex's apartment . . .

Lying in a satin sheet heaven, Christian gazed into total darkness as tears streamed down her face. She'd spent hours in bed laden with guilt over the failure of her marriage.

She sat upright, pulled up her knees, then hugged them against her chest. As her depression deepened, she glanced at the phone and contemplated calling home. Maybe it would force Jordan to talk. Was he angry—upset? Hell, did he even give a damn?

Christian laid her head against her knees and gently rocked back and forth. She'd never experienced pain like this before. She'd always carried the hope that they'd work out their differences. Tired of thinking, she rubbed her head. Shifting her weight, she swung her legs over the side of the bed. Sleep was the furthest thing from her mind. She pulled on her robe and stood.

Careful not to wake Alex in the next room, she slid through the door and tiptoed her way toward the kitchen. As she rounded a corner, she stopped.

"Great minds think alike," Christian teased, entering the kitchen.

Alex nodded and plowed another scoop of Double Fudge ice cream into her mouth.

Christian retrieved a spoon from the drawer.

"What are you doing up at three in the morning?" Alex wiped her mouth.

"I couldn't sleep. What about you?"

"Pretty much the same. You know how much I hate flying."

"With all the traveling you do, I can't believe you still have that phobia."

"If only you knew." Alex shoved in another scoop.

Christian joined her and dug her own spoon into the carton. "This reminds me of college."

"The more things change, the more they stay the same."

Christian moaned as she enjoyed the dessert's rich taste. "This is heaven on earth."

"Definitely."

"But what I can't get over is how you maintain your figure."

"I work out like a madwoman, that's how. Modeling demands perfection. But my love for this stuff borders on obsession."

"I carry every inch of this ice cream on my hips, but I don't care."

"You go, girl."

Christian thought for a moment, then asked,

"Do you think that maybe Jordan hates that I've put on a little weight?"

"Girl, please. Jordan may be a lot of things, but he's not shallow."

Christian smiled. "Thanks. I guess I needed to hear that."

They remained silent while they enjoyed their late night snack.

"Why didn't he stop me?" Christian finally asked. She laid her spoon down and leaned back in the chair. "I'd hoped I was wrong about everything." Tears pooled in her eyes. "I did everything I was supposed to do."

"Humph! That's your problem."

"What do you mean?"

"I mean, you completely dropped everything you loved to be this wife-of-the-decade or something."

"That's not true," Christian defended.

"Kid everyone else, but don't kid yourself. I've watched you try to model yourself after his mother. Which is scary, if you ask me. That woman has to be the queen socialite of Georgia. I mean, come on."

"I just wanted to blend in with—"

"What? The other millionaire's wives? I think you've forgotten that Jordan fell in love with you, and not this person you're trying to create."

Offended, Christian crossed her arms and stared at her friend. "You're saying this is all my fault?"

Alex stopped eating. "I'm not saying it's anyone's fault. I just think your problems could be solved with a better line of communication and perhaps some counseling."

"Since when are you the queen of advice? What about you and Malcolm?"

"That's different."

"How's that?"

"I caught him with another woman. I told him to go to hell, and that was all the communication we needed."

"You know he's still in love with you."

"That's his problem."

She didn't believe her, but from the stubborn set of Alex's jaw Christian knew her friend wasn't going to listen to anything she had to say in Malcolm's defense.

"Have you ever thought that maybe Jordan *wants* this divorce?"

"Chris—"

"It's a possibility." She pushed up from the table and paced the floor. "Maybe he found someone else."

"Hardly. That man worships you."

"He has a funny way of showing it." She thought some more. "What about—"

Alex shook her head. "Don't say it."

"There's no other explanation. I thought of everything else. It all comes back to one thing."

"Stop blaming yourself," Alex snapped, jumping up from' the table. "Jordan isn't shallow, and you know that."

"I'd lost one breast to cancer, Alex. And we

haven't been able to have children, despite taking every fertility drug known to mankind. What else am I suppose to think?"

"Chris—"

"Hear me out." Her voice quivered. How long can you expect a man of Jordan's stature to wait to have children?"

Alex slapped her hands against her hips. "You're so damn determined to punish yourself every day of your life for something you don't have. Why can't you take a look at what you *do* have?"

"He loves children, and I'm denying him that one pleasure. One day he's going to look back and regret not having any."

"And he'll hate you?"

"Yes." Tears trickled from her eyes, yet she held firm to her belief.

"There's adoption," Alex countered. "Why haven't you guys pursued that option?"

"You know we've talked about it. But we kept hoping that the next fertility drug would work. Then somehow the idea was put on the back burner. The next thing we knew, fifteen years had flown by." She shook her head. "You know I'm not saying I've been miserable all this time. I'd say the first ten, eleven, years, we were happy.

"I have my magazine, and I manage to get a novel published every other year or so. And of course, Jordan has J.W. Enterprises." She thought for a moment. "But for the last three years, we've both roamed through that big house as if the other doesn't exist. It's as if we've developed separate lives."

"So, you want to leave him before he leaves you?"

"I have to." Her tears fell in earnest. "I couldn't bear that kind of rejection."

Speechless, Alex pulled her friend into her arms, and they cried together.

Jordan recoiled from the sound of the alarm clock blaring in his ear. His hand shot out from the bed and fumbled on the table to find the damn thing. Out of frustration, he grabbed the clock and sent it flying across the room. However, its crash against the wall intensified his headache.

"Good shot, sir."

Jordan peeked from under his heavy eyelids. "Clarence," he moaned.

"Good morning, sir."

"Is it?"

Clarence held out a glass of his famous hangover remedy. "I thought you might be needing this."

With extreme effort, Jordan pulled his body up and accepted the glass.

Clarence turned and picked up various discarded items sprawled across the floor. "I figured you would be in here feeling sorry for yourself."

Jordan cringed from the bitter drink before replying. "She left me."

"So it seems."

Jordan drained the rest of his drink in one brave gulp. "What in the hell do you put in this stuff? It tastes like dry leather."

"You're welcome."

Jordan shook his head at his longtime friend. Clarence had worked for the Williams family since Jordan had been a baby, and was like a second father.

"Shall I run you a bath, or do you prefer we set you outside to air out?"

He caught the twinkle in the older man's eyes. "Very funny." He swung his legs over the bed and stood. The quick motion made him nauseated. "I think I need another drink."

"Malcolm is expecting you downstairs."

He groaned.

"You had planned to sell your Opulence stock to him. Remember?"

"Damn." Jordan staggered his way to the bathroom while peeling off his clothes.

While the shower's steaming hot water massaged his skin, he relaxed. Slowly, he dipped his head down to let the water pour around his face. The throbbing in his temples hadn't eased any. He retrieved the liquid soap from the shower caddy, then scrubbed himself clean.

Christian surfaced in his mind, and her betrayal flared in his heart. She should have stayed and talked things out with him instead of walking out. What the hell had ever happened to 'for better or worse'?

A few minutes later, he dressed in matching

white slacks and shirt. The redness in his eyes remained, but with any luck Malcolm wouldn't notice.

When Jordan opened the door to the study, Malcolm stood at the bar, dressed in a gray Armani suit. The brothers mirror images often confused people. Their hair, their eyes, everything was identical except for the small scar beneath Malcolm's chin.

Jordan shoved his hands inside his pockets. "Good morning."

His brother faced him, smiling. "So she finally came to her senses and left you?"

"I've missed you, too." He ignored the sarcastic remark. "Do you mind pouring me one?"

"Judging by your eyes, I'll say you've had more than enough," Malcolm commented.

He joined his brother at the bar. "Spare me the lectures and pour."

Malcolm complied. "How are you holding up?"

He laughed, then grew serious at the sight of genuine concern on his brother's face. "How did you know about Christian?"

"Clarence told me. Besides, I saw it coming."

"I swear that man has a big mouth." He finished his drink, then reached over and poured another one. "What do you mean 'you saw it coming?' "

"You can't possibly be that naive."

Jordan propped his elbows on the corner of

the bar and clasped his head between his hands. "I forgot our anniversary."

"Again? Well, I guess that shouldn't surprise me. Didn't you forget her birthday and Valentine's Day, too?"

"You can stop at any time. I've already been crucified."

Malcolm held up his hands in surrender. "Okay. I didn't mean to upset you. Maybe I should leave."

He placed a restraining hand on Malcolm's shoulder. "I didn't mean to snap at you. I'm just edgy."

Malcolm gave an easy smile. "I understand. She broke my heart once, too. Remember?"

"Are you back for good this time?" Jordan asked.

"I'm not sure. After working in our New York office for the past decade, I wouldn't mind returning home."

Jordan grunted. "For the job, or Alex?"

His brother gulped down his drink before changing the subject. "Do you want to reschedule?"

"Nah. Did you bring the paperwork?"

Malcolm reached down, then set his briefcase on the bar. "Everything is right here." He pulled out a thick manila folder.

"Do you think we're doing the right thing?" Jordan asked.

Crossing his arms, Malcolm studied him. "Are you having second thoughts?"

"Pop's going to be pissed when he finds out.

This sale will give you controlling interest in the company."

"We're doing it for his own good. Besides, what he doesn't know can't hurt him. Besides, I believe this *is* in the company's best interest. Noah's not quite acting like himself lately."

With his elbows still propped on the bar, Jordan laid his chin against his laced fingers. "Is he okay?"

"Why don't you pick up the phone and ask him yourself?"

He wanted to. "You know as well as I do that he won't speak to me."

"When was the last time you tried?"

Jordan shrugged. "About a year ago. He hung up the moment he knew it was me on the line instead of you." His heart ached from the memory. "After a while, you learn not to set yourself up for that kind of rejection." He thought of Christian and added bitterly. "And sometimes it comes, anyway."

"Sorry, Bro."

"Yeah, well, it's no big deal," he lied.

Malcolm exhaled. "Pop can be very stubborn when he wants to be. But why don't we worry about all of this when the time comes?" He slid his hands inside his pockets. "Look. I'm as apprehensive as you are about this, but Opulence is as much as our heritage as it is Noah's. The company has been around for nearly a hundred years. We have every right to protect it."

"But this seems so underhanded." Jordan locked gazes with his brother. "He's our father."

"This is business."

"I don't like this. Hell, fifteen years ago, you could have cared less about this company."

"Times have changed. I care now. If you want to play point the finger—you walked away from it."

Jordan's jaw clenched as the brothers fell into a heated silence. Then, without another word, he signed the papers.

Christian rolled over to stare up at the clock. It was noon. She'd slept through the morning. Gathering her strength, she pulled herself out of bed.

Once she made it to the vanity in the bathroom, she studied herself in the mirror. Her hair sprawled across her head, while her eyes were red and puffy. She looked exactly how she felt.

She washed her face as she reminisced about the times she shared with Alex. They'd been friends since the first day of kindergarten. Alex had been the class clown, and Christian too shy to talk to people. Together, they were the odd couple, but somehow a friendship started and had lasted for over thirty years.

Christian pulled her hair into a tight bun and applied her makeup. She stopped short at the sight of her naked fingers.

"Chris?"

"I'm in here."

Dressed in a honey-brown pantsuit, Alex entered the bathroom. "Did you oversleep, too?"

"Hell, we were up until six-thirty."

"I know. Now I'm running late for the airport. Help yourself to anything, and I'll give you a call later."

The phone rang, and Alex quickly went to answer it.

You'll never guess who's on the phone for you," Alex said, reentering the bathroom.

Her eyes beamed with hope.

"Not him."

Christian's shoulder slumped. "Then who is it?"

"Your grandmother."

"What?" She jumped from her chair and went to pick up the phone from her bedroom. "Hello? Bobby?"

Alex followed. "I left an extra key on the kitchen counter."

"Hold on a sec, Bobby." She laid the phone down, then gave Alex a hug. "You take care of yourself and call me when you make it to California."

"Promise me something," Alex said, pulling away.

"What's that?"

"That you won't make any rash decisions before talking with Jordan."

She lowered her gaze.

"Chris," Alex warned.

"Okay, I promise."

"I'll call you later." Alex left her bedroom and Christian returned to the phone.

"Hello?"

"What's going on?" Her grandmother's boisterous voice caused her to hold the phone away from her ear. I called your house this morning and Clarence told me that you moved out."

"Clarence has a big mouth."

"Don't change the subject, dear. What is going on? Why have you moved out?"

She searched for the right words, but knew there was nothing she could say that would please her grandmother.

"Are you there?"

"Yes, I'm still here."

"Well?"

"It's a long story. I don't know where to start." A thought occurred to her. "How did you know where to find me?"

"Are you kidding? You always run to Alex whenever you're troubled. You ran away from home four times, and each time you went to Alex's house."

Christian laughed.

"This also tells me that you want to be found. Jordan probably knows where you are, too."

Heartache settled in her before she could reply. "Jordan hasn't tried to contact me, and he probably won't."

"Nonsense."

The front doorbell rang. It was probably for

Alex, but after the third ring, she decided she needed to answer it. "Bobby, there's someone at the door. Can I call you back?"

"Christian, I'm not finished talking with you."

The doorbell rang again.

"I know. I promise I'll call you back."

Sighing heavily into the phone, Bobby gave in. "All right."

"Love you. Bye." She pulled her robe straps tight and raced to answer the door.

"I'm coming."

The bell rang again.

She swung open the door and froze in her tracks. "Jordan," she whispered, astonished.

He smiled. "Close. Try Malcolm."

Four

Christian stood motionless in the doorway. At the sight of the small scar beneath Malcolm's cleft chin, her heart dropped in disappointment. *Of course, he wouldn't come.*

"Aren't you going to invite me in?"

Malcolm's gallant smile and pleasant disposition made her recall her manners. She tightened her robe belt, then stepped back to allow him entry. "Forgive me, please come on in." Once he entered, she closed the door behind him. As she faced him, many questions plagued her mind.

He made a semicircle as he looked around the high-rise apartment. "Nice place." He slid his hands into his pockets and nodded in approval.

"What are you doing here?"

"To tell you the truth, I'm not sure." His dark, penetrating gaze held her curious one.

"Did you come to see Alex?"

Sadness ghosted across his features and settled in his eyes. "What happened between Alex and

me ended a long time ago." A note of regret
lingered in his voice.

"We ended longer than that," she reminded
him softly.

He smiled, the gesture never quite reaching his
eyes. "I didn't come to fight. Would you like me
to leave?"

"No." She closed her eyes and shook her head.
"I'm sorry. I'm just a little—"

"There's no need to apologize. The truth is,
when I left Jordan this morning I came to see
how you're holding up."

Christian changed the subject. "Are you back
in Atlanta for good?"

Malcolm welcomed the change. "Only time will
tell. Noah and I decided I'm needed here while
Opulence is preparing a new campaign."

Pivoting, she placed a hand against her neck
and massaged its building tensions. "So, you've
talked with Jordan this morning?" She failed at
sounding indifferent.

"I left him about an hour ago." With a lop-
sided grin, he added, "I figured you had come
here."

Christian raised a questioning brow.

"You and Alex are inseparable," he answered
confidently, then rocked on his heels.

If Malcolm could guess where she was, why
hadn't her own husband? She hid her distress.
"How is he?" she couldn't help but ask.

At his long pause, she faced him again.

He removed his hand from his pocket to rub

it across the side of his chin, as if deep in thought. "I wish I could say he's fine and is holding up." He locked gazes with her again. "But the truth is—he's miserable. He looked as if he'd spent the night in a liquor bottle."

"I wish I could say I'm sorry to hear that," Christian said. In her heart, relief settled. Jordan *had* been affected. Perhaps there was still hope.

Her mind raced a mile a minute before she remembered Malcolm. "Would you like something to drink?" she asked, walking past him to enter the living room.

He followed. "No, actually I would love it if you could join me for lunch."

She stopped.

"It's not what you think," Malcolm said before she could turn toward him. "I figured you might need to talk, that's all."

She spun around and assessed him. Malcolm, her dear friend, had showed her nothing but kindness over the years, despite their rocky break up years ago.

"I appreciate your concern. I really do, but—"

Malcolm held up his hand. "I understand." He looked around and appeared to be at a loss for words before finally asking, "Are you leaving him?"

Christian glanced heavenward. That was the question she'd spent the last month contemplating, and she wasn't any closer to an answer. "I . . . think it might be the best thing for both of us."

"You're lying."

Her eyes widened.

"But I can't tell whether it's to me . . . or to yourself." He held her gaze.

Stunned, speechless, she evaluated his words.

"Won't you reconsider having lunch with me?" he offered again.

She looked into his kind face and wished it didn't resemble her husband's. The similarity was too much for her to handle. Yet, Malcolm's thoughtfulness prevailed.

"Give me a few minutes to get ready." She smiled.

His smile broadened. "Great. How about Mick's in Underground?"

"My favorite place." Christian left to get ready.

"Great."

Within minutes, she'd dressed in a white, sleeveless jumpsuit and had pulled her hair up into a tight bun. Satisfied with her appearance, she joined Malcolm.

"This is a fabulous place," Malcolm said, staring into an original Jacob Lawrence painting. "Alex always had an eye for art."

"She does have an exceptional talent. You should see some of her sketches. They're really good."

"I don't doubt it. How is she doing? I haven't seen her in years."

The despondency in his voice tugged at her heart. "Oh, she's doing great, still busy as ever. She left this morning for California."

"I'm impressed. Every time I see her face on a magazine cover, I can't believe she's the same bossy girl I met at an Opulence photo shoot."

Christian wished there were something she could do to help the two people she loved resolve their feud. It was obvious the couple were meant for each other. Well, obvious to everyone but to them.

He smiled and offered her his arm. "Are you ready to go?"

"Yeah. Let me just grab the keys from the kitchen." She returned quickly. "I'm ready."

The phone rang.

"It's probably for Alex. I'll let the answering machine pick up," Christian said, then walked out of the apartment.

Jordan slammed the phone down when he reached Alex's answering machine. He dropped back into the leather chair as he glanced around angrily. The cluttered mess reminded him of his neglected work. And for the first time, he didn't care.

The courage he'd mustered to make the phone call had vanished, and he was left feeling discouraged. One thing he knew was that he didn't want a divorce. There was no way he could make it without her. There was no way that he'd even try. There had to be a way for them to work out their differences.

Clarence had told him of Christian's whereabouts, but it wasn't necessary. He knew exactly where she'd gone.

Pinching the bridge of his nose, he was ready to give up and just show up at Alex's door on his knees and beg for forgiveness.

Then he had an idea.

He'd show up dressed in a black tuxedo, and as he entered the apartment he'd arrange for a violinist to follow. He'd have roses brought in, along with a catered romantic dinner. Then he'd wait until the appropriate time and ask her to marry him again. *A second wedding. Yes, that's what I'll do.*

Clarence knocked and entered.

Jordan looked up.

"Sorry to disturb you, but your mother is here to see you."

"No. Tell her—"

"Jordan, dear, Clarence told me the news." Dressed in a bright, lemon-colored sundress with a matching hat, Rosa rushed around her son's desk.

He stood and cut his gaze toward Clarence, who in turn retained his stern expression.

"It's not his fault, dear. I had an engagement with Christian today, and I was wondering why she didn't show."

He leaned down as his mother rounded the desk to give him a quick peck on the check.

Clarence left the room.

"I hate to be the one to say I told you so, but I did. You should have never married that girl.

I told you she was no good, didn't I?" she chastised.

"Mama, not now."

"And why not now? That woman has done nothing but destroy this family. She fooled Malcolm once, and now you. It's a painful lesson to learn, but it's best that you cut your losses and move on."

He smiled despite the turmoil she stirred within him. "Mom, she did *not* destroy the family. Malcolm and I resolved our differences years ago. We're great friends. Malcolm and Christian's breakup wasn't solely her fault. I played a big part in what happened."

Rosa removed her hat and shook her head at Jordan. "Nonsense. That woman had woven a web so tight around the two of you that you couldn't see straight. But she never fooled me. I'm happy it's over with. Now we can finally get on with our lives."

"I thought you were going to try to get along with her."

She laughed, and took a vacant seat. "I played my part in trying to maintain an impossible relationship. I'm glad it's over."

He fell silent for a moment before replying, "I want her back."

Rosa turned and stared at her son. As if she recognized his sincerity, she tilted her head up in indignation. "Son, let her go." Her eyes implored him.

He turned away. "I can't. I love her. You have to understand that."

"I had hoped the reason you'd spent so much time away was because you were losing interest."

"Is that the new gossip you've been spreading through the country club this week?"

"That's ridiculous!"

He heard her jump to her feet.

Her voice filled with outrage. "How dare you accuse me of such—"

Jordan faced her. His hardened expression silenced her. "Do you think I don't know how you've tried to make Christian's life a living hell at that club? For years, she didn't want to participate because she didn't fit in. And after listening to this side of you, I know you had a lot to do with it."

Rosa's gaze wavered. "How can you blame me for feeling the way I do? I can't remember the last time I had my family sit down at one table to enjoy a meal together." She grabbed her purse and held Jordan's gaze with tear-filled eyes. "I just want things to be the way they were. Is that such a crime?"

"The problem is between me and Dad. You know that. He won't forgive me for deserting Opulence, despite the fact that Malcolm's doing wonders for the company."

"Give him a chance. If you ask for forgiveness, everything will be fine."

"I haven't done anything wrong!"

"Jordan—"

"Mama, please. This is a dead-end subject." He watched his mother's lips tremble as if she wanted to say something else. Instead, she turned and left his office.

He hung his head in defeat.

The phone rang and Jordan raced to answer it.

"Jordan Williams."

"What are you still doing at home?" his secretary, Charlotte, asked. "Mr. Coleman is waiting for you."

Jordan slumped into his chair. "Mr. Coleman?"

"Your one o'clock appointment. Remember?"

He shook his head. "I forgot." He glanced at the clock. "Damn, it's one-thirty. Charlotte, apologize for my absence and try to set up another appointment."

"Will do. Shall I cancel all your appointments today?"

Jordan hesitated. He needed to find Christian, but his company's new project was already on a tight schedule. "What do I have on the calendar?"

"A late lunch with Mr. Glover to go over the programmer status reports."

"Okay. I'll keep that appointment. Reschedule the rest. Where is the meeting?"

"Let me see."

He waited as she shuffled through papers.

"Oh, here it is. You're to meet him at Mick's in Underground."

Five

Elliott took the last drag from his cigarette in hopes of calming his shattered nerves. How had he gotten into this mess? His answer: for the money. For the amount of money he made, he doubted that anyone would walk away.

"Do we have a deal?" the deep, husky voice asked over the phone line.

Elliott hesitated. This act of betrayal turned his stomach. "Have I ever let you down?"

The voice laughed. "I knew we could depend on you. I will let Mr. Andrews know he has nothing to worry about."

"Before you do that, when can I expect my first payment?"

"Nothing's changed. We'll deposit half into the usual account first thing tomorrow. The rest will be deposited when the merchandise is received."

Sounded simple enough. "Good. I'll contact you when I have the goods to deliver." He ended the call, but not before guilt settled. What he was about to do could cost him more than his friendship with Jordan Williams. It could also destroy J.W. Enterprises.

Malcolm told Christian about Opulence's new developments over lunch. "Our stock has sky-rocketed during the last quarter. That has every-one breathing a little easier around the office."

"That's great. I bet Noah is proud of you." She smiled.

He frowned. "I don't know about that. His heart has always been set on Jordan running the company."

"But you're doing a wonderful job."

"The bottom line is, I'm not Jordan."

She averted her eyes.

"I'm sorry," he apologized when he realized what he'd said.

She gave him a weak smile. "It's all right. You know, sometimes I can't help but feel guilty. I know it was a long time ago, but I—" She blushed as she searched for the right words.

Malcolm grasped her hand. "You're right. It was a long time ago. We've both moved on. I have no hard feelings. And neither should you. Whether you and my brother know it or not, you're meant for each other."

"I don't know about that." She pulled her hand back.

"Well, I do. Do you believe in soul mates?"

Her eyes widened. "What?"

"Come on. You know what I mean. Two souls destined to be together. Soul mates."

Christian smiled. "Yes. I know what it means. I guess I'm just a little surprised to hear it from you."

"What? Men can't believe in such things?"

"Well, yeah. I mean . . . Actually, I don't know what I mean."

"Oh, I get it. You didn't think *I* believed in it." He laughed. "I might have deserved that comment at one time in my life."

"What changed your mind?"

His smile faded. "Alex."

She sobered.

His gaze lowered. "You know, a long time ago I promised myself I'd win her back." He looked up. "I still love her."

"I'm sorry," was all she could think to say.

"There's no need to be sorry. The bottom line is, I screwed up. And I know I'm only lying to myself to believe things would ever change."

"Why don't you talk to her?"

"She won't talk to me." He shook his head. "I guess being at her apartment today brought back some old memories. There was a part of me that hoped she'd be there."

"So, I was your excuse to see her?"

"Sorry."

This time, Christian reached for his hand. "There's no need for you to be sorry. I just wish there was something I could do."

* * *

Jordan parked outside Mick's, then rushed to straighten his tie. When he looked at his reflection, Christian's image floated in his mind.

He pulled his gaze from the mirror and stepped out of the car. He needed to concentrate on the matter at hand. But when he slid his hands into his pockets and withdrew his wife's rings, a sudden confidence lifted his spirits. After tonight, everything would be back to normal.

He'd managed to have Charlotte arrange a special candlelight dinner for two at Alex's apartment. No doubt it would be the perfect catalyst to win Christian over, so that they could get on with their lives. All he had to do was make sure he arrived promptly at eight.

He returned the rings to his pocket and hurried into the restaurant. Once inside, he scanned the room, hoping to spot his client.

Instead, his gaze centered on a table near the back of the restaurant.

Eyes wide, Jordan felt as if his heart swelled in his chest. What in the hell was Christian doing here with Malcolm?

Six

Jordan's eyes blazed as a sharp pang of betrayal trickled through him.

Malcolm kissed Christian's hand, then reeled back with a hearty laugh.

Jordan's temper reached a boiling point, and was ready to explode. He ignored the voice in his head warning him of their innocence. He only listened to his mounting anger.

Christian laughed, then a sudden prickly sensation raced down her spine. When she turned, her gaze crashed with her husband's.

Her mouth opened, but before she could speak, Jordan's hand snaked out and grabbed Malcolm by the collar, jerking him out of his chair.

"You sorry son of a—"

"Jordan, no!" She jumped to restrain his arm, but it was too late. His punch sent Malcolm sprawling backward.

He flipped over his chair and landed hard against the wooden floor.

She rushed to his side with her eyes wide with horror. "Malcolm. Are you all right?"

"I don't think it's broken," he moaned, touching his nose.

"Stand up and I'll fix that for you."

"Jordan!" Christian turned her accusing eyes toward him.

His stomach lurched at their loving display. His mother's warning echoed through his head.

Christian stood and noticed all eyes were on them. Angrily, she whispered. "What in the hell has gotten into you?"

He took a threatening step forward. "I'll not be made a fool of."

"You're doing a great job of that on your own."

Malcolm shook his head, then held out his hand to prevent Jordan from coming any closer. "This isn't what you think."

"I trusted both of you," Jordan continued. "How long has this been going on?"

"What?" Christian's eyes grew large. "What are you accusing me of?"

"A month? A year? How long have you been cheating behind my back?"

Christian delivered a powerful slap to his right cheek, then ignored her stinging hand as she glared at him. "How *dare* you."

His eyes narrowed. "How long?"

"Jordan, man. You need to calm down. Nothing is going on between us." Malcolm stepped between them. "Can't we just sit here and resolve this peacefully."

"Not here," a man said behind them. "I'm the manager, and I want you all to leave."

Jordan's jaw twitched in anger as he ignored the manager's request. "You expect me to believe you after what I saw?"

He focused most of his attention on Christian. "Do you enjoy bouncing from one brother to another? Are you having a good time playing us both as fools?"

"That's enough, Jordan. I've already told you there's nothing going on," Malcolm snapped.

Tears stung Christian's eyes, but she refused to let them fall. "I hate you," she whispered through trembling lips.

She snatched her purse from the table and walked around Malcolm, but Jordan refused to allow her to escape.

"Don't make me call the police," the persistent manager threatened.

"I'll give you your divorce, but you won't get one red cent from me." He hissed the words for only her to hear.

Shock couched by disappointment ricocheted through her body. "I don't give a damn about your money," she announced when she found her voice again. "I just want to get away from you."

"At least now I know the truth."

"You wouldn't know the truth if it bit you on the ass." She yanked her arm back, and stormed away. Her face flushed with humiliation, she passed through the lunch crowd and exited the restaurant without a backward glance.

"Christian, wait," Malcolm called out. He threw some money on the table and ran after her, leaving Jordan to deal with the gossiping witnesses.

"Wait up," Malcolm shouted. When he caught up with her, she continued to charge down the sidewalk.

"Let me take you back to Alex's apartment," he offered.

Trembling with rage, Christian stopped and looked at him. Tears fell freely now as she struggled to gather her senses. "I think I'd rather walk."

"I don't feel comfortable with you walking back."

She closed her eyes and allowed the slight afternoon breeze to calm her down. In reality, the light wind offered little help with her temper. The increasing humidity warned her of how uncomfortable the long walk would be, but still she refused the offer.

"Thank you, but I need time to think." She gave him a friendly peck on the cheek. "I'll be fine," she assured him, then walked away.

Malcolm shook his head at her retreating figure. Turning around, he set his mind on straightening out his brother.

* * *

Noah's plastic smile melted the moment his office door closed, leaving him alone. He had survived the last meeting of the day, but only by God's mercy. Listening to Mr. Chin's profit and loss ramblings was enough to do anyone in.

A deep sigh relieved much of his tension, but his heart remained heavy. As his weary gaze centered on a picture of Rosa, the love of his life, he smiled.

Next, he glanced at another photograph on the far in of his desk. Conflicting emotions surfaced once again. Though it had been years, he still experienced a strong sense of hurt and betrayal whenever he looked at Jordan.

It had been years since he'd uttered a word to his eldest son, even though in the back of his mind he knew the grudge he harbored bordered on the ridiculous. But damned if he could help the way he felt.

There wasn't a day that passed when Rosa didn't plan or scheme to get him to bury the hatchet, but he refused her at every turn.

Shame churned within him.

He'd hoped J.W. Enterprises would be nothing more than a phase, and then Jordan would come running back to the family business. But it never happened.

Then, before he knew it, his disappointment had turned into anger, and pride prevented him from taking the first step to bridge the gap.

He stood from his chair, feeling more tired than normal. Each day his struggle with depression grew worse. It didn't matter how many times he'd reminded himself of how lucky in life he'd been, or of how much he loved his wife, or of how proud he was of Malcolm's accomplishment with the company. Nothing really mattered anymore.

Pulling out his stashed bottle of Scotch, he took a swig. The jolt of alcohol brought another smile to his face. He shouldn't be drinking, he realized, but he knew of nothing else that could quite take the pain away.

"You have some nerve." Malcolm snatched his brother by the shoulder.

Jordan spun on his heel. "I think it's best you stay away from me right now, Mal. I'm on the verge of beating the hell out of you."

He ignored the warning. "Why did you humiliate her like that?"

Venom laced Jordan's voice. "If anyone should be asking questions, it should be me. Such as, what in the hell were you doing cozying in the back of a restaurant with *my* wife? Was your little visit this morning some sick way of gloating?"

"Gloating? What are you talking about? Since when is it a crime to take my sister-in-law out to lunch?"

"I know you're not going to stand there and try to deny it. I saw the way you were looking at her."

As an alternative to landing a punch across his

brother's jaw, Malcolm jabbed his fists into his pockets. "Now I know you've lost your damn mind."

Jordan's heart tightened. The possibility of Christian and Malcolm rekindling old feelings pained him. "Just tell me one thing, and please be honest with me." His voice dropped an octave. "How long has this been going on?" Careful to keep his torrid emotions from surfacing, he waited through the ensuing silence.

"I'm not even going to dignify that with an answer." Malcolm's irritation caused a nerve to twitch along his temple. "Christian loves you. She still loves you. Though at this moment I can't fathom why. If you'd only open your eyes, you'd see that for yourself."

Relief swept through Jordan.

Malcolm refused to let the matter drop. "You know, everything doesn't revolve around J.W. Enterprises. Don't get me wrong. I understand your drive to make it number one. At times, I even admire your commitment. But at what cost are you willing to make that happen? Is it worth your marriage?"

Laughter rumbled from Jordan's chest, but the joviality died in his eyes. "Are you a marriage counselor now? A man who can't even spell commitment, let alone know the definition, wants to tell me how to save my marriage?"

"It doesn't take a rocket scientist to know you're screwing it up."

Jordan jerked around in time to see his lunch appointment arrive.

"Mr. Glover," he called out to the older man's direction.

"That's right, Bro. Go take care of business. It's only your life that's falling apart." Malcolm sneered.

The razor-sharp retort found its mark.

Jordan straightened his shoulders. His anger had somewhat dissipated, but his heartache nearly consumed him as he realized everything his brother had said . . . was true.

Seven

Christian stopped along the sidewalk and cursed the hot sun. She replayed the scene at Mick's for the thousandth time with a myriad of emotions. Jordan had, at least, shown a reaction. It just wasn't the one she wanted. He'd made it clear he wanted to go through with the divorce.

She struggled to forget their plans for the future, or the promises they'd made, especially the promise to stay together forever. The hardest thing was not to blame herself.

Christian opened her purse and pulled out a card—Barnell & Hernandez, Attorneys-at-Law. She'd put off the inevitable for too long. She looked around and spotted a cab. Frantically, she waved it down.

The cab pulled up and she jumped in.

"Take me to fifty-three hundred Peachtree Street, please," she instructed, then turned to look out the window.

When she arrived at a small business complex, her stomach was tangled in knots.

After the cab drove off, she lingered outside

the building, withering beneath the blazing sun. Finally, she forced herself to enter.

"May I help you?"

Christian smiled as she approached a pretty, blue-eyed receptionist. She looked down at her card and asked, "Is there any way I can speak with Abraham Barnell or Keith Hernandez?"

"Do you have an appointment"

Christian's smile weakened. "No, this is rather sudden."

"Just one moment."

"Thank you." Christian turned and took a deep breath.

She counted to ten in an attempt to calm her nerves.

"Ma'am? May I have your name?"

"Christian Williams."

The receptionist repeated her name into the headgear, then quickly returned her attention to her. "Mr. Barnell can see you before his three-thirty appointment You can take the elevator." She pointed toward the end of the hall. "Go to the third floor, then look for suite three thirty six. Mary will help you from there."

"Thank you." Christian walked to the open elevator bay on weakened knees. She couldn't believe she was doing this. The bell chimed all too soon when she arrived on the third floor. She found the suite and took a deep breath before entering.

"Mrs. Williams?"

Christian turned toward a dark, beautiful woman with a friendly smile. "Yes?"

"I'm Mary Stevens, Mr. Barnell's assistant."

"Hello."

"Can I get you to fill out a few forms before Mr. Barnell sees you?"

"Of course." She accepted a clipboard that held a thick stack of papers in place. She sat down and began completing the forms, which seemed to ask everything but the color of her underwear. When she finished, her fingers ached.

"Just follow me, Mrs. Williams." Mary smiled.

"Please call me Christian."

Mary took her to an office decorated beautifully with cherry and oak furniture. It reminded her of Jordan's home office.

"Have a seat. Mr. Barnell will be in shortly."

Christian sat in a vacant chair in front of the desk and took note of the different certificates hanging on the walls. The bookshelves were packed with handsome, bound law books.

When the door opened, a handsome, older man entered the room. He reminded her of Dylan, her grandmother's fiancé, with his head full of gray, cropped hair and deep wrinkles around his eyes.

"Sorry to keep you waiting. How are you doing today, Mrs. Williams?"

"Just fine," she lied.

He sat behind his desk. "It says here you want to file for a divorce." He peered through silver-rimmed glasses at the stack of papers she'd just completed.

"That's correct. A friend of mine highly recommended your office. A Ms. Rogers."

"Oh, Emily referred you. That's good, that's good." He viewed the documents again. "Do you mind if I ask why?"

"Irreconcilable differences."

"I see." He scribbled something down on a notepad. "You've been married for fifteen years. Is that correct?"

"Yes."

"There are no children?" He flipped through the paperwork.

Her heart skipped a beat. "No."

Barnell leaned back in his chair and studied her. She shifted and avoided making eye contact.

"Does your husband know you're here?" His voice took on a parental tone.

"He knows about the divorce, if that's what you mean."

"And what does he have to say?"

"Nothing."

"Nothing?"

She met his gaze bravely. "He said I won't get one red cent from him."

Barnell smiled. "Really? And just who is your husband?"

"Jordan Williams, president and founder of J.W. Enterprises."

"The computer software company?"

"That's the one."

Barnell wrote more on his notepad. "Is there any foul play involved?"

"Foul play?"

"Is there another woman, or are you seeing someone else?"

"I don't think . . . no, there isn't anyone else." Christian frowned.

"What about you?"

"No."

"You're an editor and a novelist."

"Yes, I run a magazine called *Nuwoman,*" she answered nervously.

"I see. Did you sign a prenuptial agreement?"

"No, but I don't want anything. I just want out."

Barnell sat his pen down. "Mrs. Williams, have you thought about this? Are you having any second thoughts?"

Christian made eye contact as she gathered her courage. "No. I've made up my mind. I want this divorce."

Jordan's mood hadn't improved since he left Mick's. He barked orders at Charlotte until she started barking back, but he didn't care. He just wanted to bury himself with work and forget everything. However, as time passed, the scene at lunch replayed in his mind, each time in more vivid detail.

When it became difficult to concentrate on work, he left the office at five o'clock, for the first time in years. He regretted his decision the moment he found himself in bumper-to-bumper traffic.

By the time he made it home, he was in a worse mood. He retrieved a bottle of Jack Daniels from the bar in the parlor and headed up to his room.

The house seemed cold and empty. Once upstairs, he poured his first drink. He remembered walking into Mick's and seeing Christian laughing. When was the last time he'd seen her laugh like that?

He thought of her smiling at Malcolm, and couldn't remember the last time she smiled at him that way, either. He was on his sixth drink, or maybe it was the seventh, when he remembered Malcolm kissing her hand.

He pulled her rings from his pocket and stared at them. Like hell he'd give her a divorce. Maybe he'd kidnap her, and take her so far from Atlanta she'd forget how to spell it. It was a good plan, and it sounded better with each drink.

Alex's heart sank. She closed her eyes and prayed that they were deceiving her. Then she chanced another look at the now vivid blue strip on the home pregnancy test. *Positive.* "Oh, God."

She tossed the fifth test into the bathroom's wastebasket and lowered her body onto the cold, hard, tile floor. *What am I going to do?* Tears brimmed in her eyes. Her hands trembled as she brought them up to massage her temples.

A baby.

A mother.

Nausea washed over her, and within seconds her head hovered above the toilet as she emptied the contents of her stomach. When she came up for air, her throbbing temples had turned into a full-scale migraine.

A knock sounded at the door, but to Alex it sounded more like her visitor was trying to tear the door down.

"Just a minute," she managed to say, but pulling herself off the bathroom's cold floor seemed impossible.

Another knock ensued.

"I said I was coming," she shouted, then cringed from the volume of her voice. Weak, she forced one foot in front of the other and made her way to the door.

Her insistent visitor rapped louder.

Alex pulled the door open in a jerk, then froze. "Robert."

Robert Conners's easy smile dissolved. "Are you okay? You look like hell."

"It's great to see you, too." Her tone contradicted her statement.

"Mind if I come in?" He entered without waiting for a response.

"Sure. Make yourself at home," she replied sarcastically.

At six-three, Robert Conners dominated the

room. His midnight complexion and smoldering eyes still sent her heart in flight, but she quickly regained her composure. There was a time when just one look from him left her weak-kneed.

Times had changed.

"What are you doing here?"

His gaze turned curious. "I'm not welcome here anymore?"

'No' crested the tip of her tongue, but instead she took a deep breath. "You know what I mean. We said everything six weeks ago."

"I thought—after you'd calmed down and had time to think things over—you'd have changed your mind."

"Hardly."

"Now come on, Baby." He stepped forward.

She took two steps back. "Don't 'Baby' me." She turned away and crossed her arms. When the room spun around her, she reached out to steady her weight with a nearby chair.

"Are you all right?"

"I'm fine," she recited automatically, then faced him. *I'm pregnant with your child* nearly escaped her lips. "I think you should go."

Anger flashed in Robert's eyes. "Will you stop being so damn difficult? Nothing has to change." He moved forward. "I still love you."

His words stabbed her heart. "Don't say that." She closed her eyes and forbade her tears to fall.

"You love me, too. You just won't allow yourself to admit it."

Alex's eyes snapped open. "You have some

nerve. How can you stand there and speak to me. You used me."

"That's not true. I've never felt this way about any woman." His voice lowered seductively. "I need you back in my life. Nothing has to change. I know I should have told you the truth, but I couldn't risk losing you."

She shook her head, forbidding his words to take root in her heart. "We can never go back to the way we were. And if you'd be honest with yourself, you'd know that I'm right. You deliberately led me on for almost a year. *A year.*" Tears slid from her eyes as she drew in a shaky breath. "I can never forgive you for that. I'm not even sure that I want to try."

Robert slid his hands into his pockets and shifted his weight. "There's no need for you to be so cold, Alex."

"You didn't have to be so cruel." She turned and walked back to the front door.

"I'm not leaving," Robert's voice thundered. "Not until we settle this." His eyes implored her when she faced him again. "We can make this work, I just know we can."

Alex placed her hand against her stomach. She had too much at stake. Her chaotic emotions warred against one another while reason seemed to escape her.

Robert pulled his body erect as his temper got the best of him. "Damn it, Alex. What more do you want from me?"

A sad smile curved her lips. "That's just it. I

don't want anything from you. What I wanted you're incapable of giving. And if I stay, I'll be cheating, myself."

"Don't you love me?"

She nodded. "But I love myself more." She opened the door, and once again they locked gazes. "Go home to your wife."

Eight

"I hate him," Christian shouted as she slammed the apartment door and then slumped back against it. Tears raced down her cheeks as she closed her eyes and admitted to herself that she could never hate Jordan.

The familiar sense of loneliness settled on her shoulders. By now, she should have had a better handle on things. But each day everything seemed harder—getting through each day, each hour.

A divorce.

It was a big step. On days like today, the notion didn't seem so inconceivable. Yet, how could she leave him when her heart, her soul, cried out for him?

Snap out of it. Christian stilled her trembling lips. How much longer would she continue to feel sorry for herself? It was high time she ended this pity party, *right*? "Right," she confirmed.

Wiping her remaining tears with the back of her hand, she pulled her body erect. She needed to start looking out for herself, start taking control of her life.

She pushed herself away from the door. Things needed to change. *She* needed to change. It was time she stopped being Mrs. Jordan Williams and made a name for herself. And she knew just the thing she needed to do first.

No sooner had she made her declaration than the doorbell rang. Curious, she opened it and was instantly floored by the sudden parade of men who carried in four large wreaths of roses.

"Mrs. Williams?"

"Yes?" Christian turned toward a well-dressed man who handed her an envelope. She opened it and pulled out a card.

> *To Christian—*
> > *Endless Love,*
> > > *Jordan.*

Hope flourished in her heart as she looked up and watched the men arrange a candlelight dinner.

I have to change, she realized, then rushed to the bedroom. She dressed in record time and struggled to compose herself in front of the mirror. She felt like a teenager waiting for her prom date.

When she returned to the living-room, the scene the men had prepared stole her breath. Wonderful aromas wafted through the air and seduced her senses. A gentleman nodded in her direction, then placed a violin beneath his chin and began to play.

She smiled. The only thing missing was Jordan.

Christian sat at the table, still relishing her surroundings, and waited for her husband to appear.

Hours later, disappointment and disbelief engulfed her as she still sat alone at the elegantly prepared table set for two. The violinist selected another song and began to play. She stared at the four wreaths of roses through a thin sheen of tears.

How could he have gone to so much trouble to prepare a romantic evening and not shown up? The concept seemed absurd. And their present situation now seemed more hopeless.

Despite everything that had happened today, a flare of hope had sparked in her heart, and she'd actually believed that maybe, just maybe, they could resolve their differences.

She was a fool.

She stood and asked the violinist to leave. When she saw sympathy in his eyes, her heart dropped.

Loneliness embraced her. Once again, it would be her companion through the night. But this time, no tears fell. No cries of injustice came from her lips. Only acceptance of her fate consoled her. And it would have to be enough.

"Our competitors are trying to convince consumers that Opulence is an old-fashioned company, with high prices, and that they offer a better cut diamond for the money." Malcolm read from his notes. "I'm asking this marketing department to go out on a limb. We need something fresh, something new."

"I'm not offended by Opulence being labeled as old-fashioned." Noah spoke from the head of the table.

Malcolm glanced up and locked gazes with his father. "It's not wise just to appeal to the older generation. I think we need to attract everyone—newlyweds as well as fiftieth anniversary couples. That's the only way we can survive."

Noah's boisterous laugh drew everyone's attention. "Opulence has been around since long before I was an itch in my father's pants. So don't talk to me about survival," he thundered.

This was going to be another long meeting. His father challenged his authority at all angles. Everyone looked from Noah to Malcolm, and waited for the usual show.

Malcolm inhaled and counted to ten. "Times are changing. We need to change with them. We've done this before, and we can do it again."

"What are you talking about? We just celebrated record sales last quarter," Noah barked.

"We're still second to Emerald Jewelers."

The twelve man marketing department nodded in agreement.

Noah became more incensed. "And what exactly are you planning to do with *my* company? Advertise half-naked women over expensive cars?

But wait, they're wearing diamonds by Opulence."

A low rumble of laughter filled the room as everyone recognized their competitor's advertising slogan.

Malcolm shook his head. "That's where these men come into play. I'm not suggesting that we sell sex or cars. The main focus is our product."

Everyone nodded, then looked to Noah to continue the debate.

He declined.

"I want a layout presented to me in two weeks. Are there any more questions?" Malcolm waited for his father to protest, but Noah remained silent. *Thank God.*

"All right, then. I'll see everyone then." Malcolm gathered his papers as everyone filed out of the room.

Noah stopped him. "I'm not sure I like your idea of changing the company's image."

Malcolm wasn't surprised. He closed his briefcase. "I know it's hard to accept change, Pop. But I firmly believe that this is what's best for the company."

"But—"

"Look, you've trusted my judgment in the past. What's changed?"

Noah fell silent.

"In the past fifteen years, have I ever let you down?"

Noah lowered his head.

Malcolm witnessed a strange look of defeat in

the way his father hunched his shoulders. If he didn't know any better, he'd swear his father had aged ten years right before his eyes. He placed a comforting hand on his shoulders. "Just trust me, Pop. I promise I won't let you down."

Noah squared his shoulders and stared at his son. Then, without another word, he turned, and walked out of the conference room.

Malcolm's gaze followed him. And for the millionth time, he worried about his father's mental health.

Noah walked to his office in long angry strides. It had taken him years to achieve Opulence's 'old-fashioned' values. Every day Malcolm made more and more decisions for the company. The employees accepted his son's authority over his, and he hated this growing feeling of uselessness.

He opened his office door to find his wife sitting behind his desk. A smile broadened across his face. "I see you like my chair." He walked over to her and placed a butterfly kiss against her cheek.

"I didn't hear you come in last night, and you left so early this morning," she offered as an explanation. "So, I decided to come and see you."

"Malcolm had a secret marketing meeting planned this morning." Noah didn't bother to hide his irritation.

"Maybe it just slipped his mind to tell you." She dismissed his paranoia and smiled sweetly at him.

Noah doubted it, but returned the favor to relax his wife. "Perhaps you're right." He kissed her again. "Now what brings you here?"

"I have some news that I've been dying to tell you. It's about Jordan and Christian."

"Oh?" Noah moved away from his desk and headed to the bar at the opposite end of the office.

"They're getting a divorce."

He halted and looked back at her. "A divorce?"

Rosa's smile brightened. "Yes."

Noah reached the bar and fixed himself a Scotch on the rocks.

"The doctor asked you to stop drinking," Rosa warned.

"I think that you and the doctor forget that I'm well over the legal drinking age."

Rosa jumped to her feet and made it to the bar before the glass touched his lips. "That's not funny. You need to take better care of yourself." She took the drink from him. "If you can't do it for yourself, then at least do it for the family."

He knew better than to try to fight with her on this. "All right." His shoulders slumped in defeat, and he went back to his desk.

She smiled in triumph as she followed him. "As I was saying—I went to see Jordan yesterday, and sure enough, Christian had moved out."

"How did you find out about this?" Noah sat behind his desk.

"Clarence."

Noah shook his head. "That man has a big mouth."

"Come on. You know Clarence adores Jordan." She carried on. "Besides, isn't this great news?"

"Frankly, I don't see where it's any of our business."

"Not any of our business? This means Jordan will come back home." Rosa's voice raised an octave.

"I don't follow you."

"Our family will be together again. With that woman out of the picture, Jordan will want to spend more time with his family."

Noah stared at Rosa and tried to understand her logic. "What did Jordan tell you?"

Rosa shrugged. "The boy is confused right now. He doesn't know what he wants."

"What did he say?"

She sighed. "He said he wants her back."

Noah pinched the bridge of his nose. "Then why are you so bubbly about a divorce?"

"Come on, honey. You know that she never loved Jordan."

"I know no such thing. And neither do you. A woman doesn't stay married to a man she doesn't love for fifteen years."

"How can you say that? Don't you want us to be a family again?"

Noah lowered his gaze. "Christian doesn't have anything to do with him not visiting. The man is stubborn, and a workaholic." He shook his head. "Two terrible traits he got from me," he ended on a note of regret.

"Then whatever it is that separated this family, I want it resolved. I'm tired of traveling across Atlanta to see Jordan. I want him to feel free to come home and share a meal with his parents." Rosa trembled as she shouted. She drained his drink in a single gulp, then waltzed back to the bar and grabbed the Scotch bottle. "Is this the only one you have here?"

He heaved his chest wearily. "Yes."

"Good." She took the bottle and grabbed her purse from his desk. She left his office, slamming the door behind her.

Noah waited a moment. Then, sensing that the coast was clear, he pulled out his second stashed Scotch bottle from his desk.

The door burst open.

Rosa marched to his desk and snatched the bottle from his hands, then stormed back out.

Noah dropped his head back, and a smile curved his lips. "Damn, she's good."

Nine

One week later

Malcolm tossed down his pen, then pushed back in his chair. "What a day." He expelled a long frustrated sigh in hopes of releasing the day's anxieties, but to no avail. Something needed to change. It was Friday night, and the only thing he had to look forward to was reading through a stack of acquisition contracts. *What a life.*

At this rate, he'd undoubtedly become like all the other men in his family—a workaholic. The thought depressed him. Once upon a time, he'd known how to relax. He remembered when it seemed he had a different woman on his arm every day of the week. Now, the only thing that occupied his time was Opulence. What had happened?

Malcolm's heart squeezed as his answer came with a beautiful image of Alexandria Cheney. He had fallen in love. Turning in his chair, he faced the window. Downtown Atlanta's various sky-rises and lights greeted him. The view often stole his breath and captured his imagination.

Alex resurfaced in his mind. How he missed her. For years she'd been his best friend, the one person he could always depend on, even when he'd confessed his love for Christian.

He frowned. What a fool he'd been not to see the love she had for him then. What a fool he'd been not to realize Alex had already stolen his heart, not Christian.

He stood from his chair and moved closer to the window. Maybe they were never meant to be together. His heart ached with denial. Why was he torturing himself? How long was he going to allow the past to haunt his future?

He sucked in a deep breath and shook his head. Reality check: after fifteen years, Alex still owned his heart, and for as long as he lived, she always would.

Looking up into the night's velvety curtain, he wondered, as he did every night, what she was doing just then.

Alex pulled her gaze from the window and closed her eyes as tears slid from her face. What was she going to do? She shook her head. For the first time in her life, she didn't have a clue.

All her life, she'd planned everything. And now . . . ?

She crossed her arms, seeking comfort from within, but no answers came. Soon she would have to leave this apartment and face the world. One thing was sure—she would have to tell Robert about the baby. It was the right thing to do. Right?

She didn't know anymore.

Entering her bedroom, she caught a glimpse of herself in the mirror and stopped.

She didn't look any different. She turned from side to side, searching for any change in her appearance. Where was that glowing skin she'd heard so much about? If anything, she looked pale.

Disappointed, Alex gave up and returned to bed—a place where she'd spent too much time lately. *Maybe I'll go out tomorrow.* Tomorrow she would talk to Robert. Tomorrow she'd make plans for the future. Dread dripped through her veins.

If she were lucky, tomorrow would never come.

She was tired; tired of worrying, tired of thinking. But questions continued to chase each other in her mind.

Why did she always fall for the wrong men?

Faded memories suddenly crystallized, and she remembered the last man she'd trusted with her heart—Malcolm Jamal Williams. Pain she'd long forgotten returned. To this day, she'd never loved a man so completely. Even now, the hurt she felt from Robert's betrayal paled in comparison to Malcolm's.

I miss him.

Alex hated the whispered confession of her

heart. As was her habit, she struggled to block out his image, but tonight it was useless.

Tonight, she remembered every detail—from the warmth of his smile to the sheer strength of his embrace. Oh, how she missed him.

She turned to her side, pulling a body-length pillow against her. Their one night of passion drifted like a dream in her mind. Suddenly, his familiar scent seemed to fill the room, and the wonderful taste of his mouth lingered on her lips.

Alex clutched the pillow tighter. Her body ached in remembrance of his touch. Desire ebbed her soul, and love reined true in her heart.

Such rapture, such joy. Those emotions were lost to her now, no matter how hard she tried to recapture them. And she'd tried with Robert. Agony and regret hastily destroyed the seductive images in her head, and an invisible scar throbbed across her heart.

Her eyes fluttered open as she rolled onto her back, and she placed a hand against her flat stomach. Now she was going to be a single mother.

She pressed her trembling lips together, forbidding her tears to fall. She was tired of crying, tired of feeling sorry for herself. Yet, she was unable to prevent either from happening.

Maybe I should call Chris. She wanted to, needed to, but what would she say? Chris had been trying to get pregnant for years.

The last thing Alex wanted was to cause her friend any unnecessary pain, but she needed to talk to someone before she went crazy. Maybe she was being silly. Chris would never give her less than a hundred percent support.

Alex sat up in bed and reached for the phone. Her mind remained blank as she waited for the connection.

"Hello."

An instant smile tilted her lips. "Hey, girl."

"Alex," Christian's voice perked. "I was worried about you. Why haven't you returned any of my calls?"

"Sorry. I guess I've been busy. You know how crazy my schedule can get. I still have that jeweler's convention to attend later this week."

An awkward silence hung over the line.

"Are you okay?"

There was no mistaking the concern in Christian's voice. Alex decided to be honest. "No."

"What is it?"

"Everything." Her control shattered. "I—I don't know how I got here."

"Dear God, what happened?"

Silence.

"Alex, don't do this to me. Do you need me to fly out there? I can get booked on the next flight."

"No." She sniffled and made an attempt to gather her courage. "Don't do that. It's just that . . . I've made a big mistake. I made several, actually. And I don't know what to do about them." She cringed at the note of desperation in her voice.

Impatient, Christian commanded, "You're scaring me. Just spit it out. What mistakes are you talking about?"

"I'm pregnant."

Silence.

Anxiety knotted in the pit of her stomach. "Are you still there?"

"Yeah." Another pause held over the line before Christian asked, "Are you sure?"

"Quite. I don't think there's an available home pregnancy test left in California." Her attempt at humor failed. "I'm not ready for this," she confessed.

"Is Robert—"

"Yes."

"Oh, Alex. I don't know what to say. But as for you not being ready, very few women think they are at first. I know you'll make a great mother. I don't think that you should view this as a bad thing."

"I didn't plan for this to happen."

Christian's soft laughter rumbled over the line. "Things don't always go as planned. You and I both should know that. I never dreamed that one day I'd file for divorce."

"Oh, Chris, I almost forgot. Here I am rambling about my own problems, and I haven't stopped to ask how you're holding up."

"I'm okay. It just feels as if someone yanked

my heart out of my chest. But I'm taking it one day at a time."

"Is there anything I can do for you?"

"No. It's over, and I have to deal with that on my own."

"Have you talked to Jordan?"

There's nothing left for us. I'm more certain about that than I've ever been."

"I'm so sorry." Alex's heart ached for her friend.

Christian sighed. "So am I."

Ten

Jordan sat at the head of the conference table, feeling the pains of another headache. "Your progress reports said that the programmers were on schedule."

Quentin nodded. "The documents I handed you yesterday were accurate at the time. But now we've stumbled onto a problem. It's going to take at least three weeks to back up and see what went wrong."

"We don't have three weeks. This software is due on the shelves by the holidays—in a few months."

"I understand that, Jordan, but our hands are tied. I can put more men on the job, but that's no guarantee that the problem will be rooted out any faster."

Jordan's gaze shifted to the other employees. Normally, he would have blown his top by now, but the residue of that morning's hangover prevented him. "Put more men on it. You have thirty days to solve the problem and get us back on schedule."

"But—"

"I think that concludes this meeting." Jordan stood from his chair, grabbed his briefcase, and stormed out of the conference room. His mind tangled with this new development. This was the last thing he needed.

He slammed the door to his office, which only intensified his throbbing headache. He went to his desk and pressed the intercom. "Charlotte, were there any calls?"

"I placed messages on your desk. And no, your wife hasn't called."

"Thanks." Jordan caught the irritation in her voice. No doubt she was still angry about his sour mood.

Seconds later, a knock sounded and the door flew open before he could reply.

"Good morning, Jordy," Michael shouted, strolling into the office.

Jordan suppressed the urge to wrap his hands around his competitor's neck for shouting. "It's Mr. Williams to you, Mikey."

Michael's bark of laughter rode Jordan's last thin nerve as he toyed with the thought of murder.

"Glad to see you still have a sense of humor."

"What are you doing here? Don't you have a company to run?"

"Everything is running smoothly down at Compucom Systems." Michael pushed his flaxen-colored hair from his eyes and smiled. "In fact, our voice-activated personal assistant software is due to hit the market a month early."

Jordan's head cleared. Their companies were developing similar software. "Oh really?"

"Sorry to be the one to break the news to you, but I thought about our long history together, and knew that you would want to be the first to hear about this, so I rushed right over."

"How considerate of you."

Michael's eyes twinkled. "I guess J.W. Enterprises will have to take a backseat this time."

"It's not over yet, my friend." Jordan bluffed.

Michael crossed his arms. "I'm amazed you consider yourself still in the race."

"J.W. Enterprises will be the first with the voice-activated personal assistant software, make no mistake about it."

"You sound rather sure of yourself. I hate to be the one to burst your bubble, but I will stop at nothing to ensure our success." Michael's attitude remained friendly.

"We'll just see about that."

Michael stood. "For years now, your company has been regarded as a reigning force in this business. Maybe it's time for another company to take the spotlight."

Jordan shook his head. "Then I guess I'll see you at the finish line." His tone declared that their chat was over.

"It's been a pleasure. I look forward to burying you and your company. The truth is—the company who comes out on top this time stands to lead the world in technology."

"I seriously doubt that Compucom Systems could lead anyone into the backyard. For such a young company, you're reaching pretty high."

Michael's neck reddened. "We'll see. Don't underestimate me on this. I *will* come out on top."

Pride prevented Jordan from backing down. "I'll see you at the finish line."

"One day, you're going to admit that you lost the best programmer you ever had."

Jordan chuckled. "I seem to recall that you left the company on your own."

"I grew tired of the glass ceiling you seem to have around here."

"As much as I would love to hear you cry injustice, I do have a company to run. The last time I checked, so did you."

Michael moved toward the door. "I think I'm going to enjoy this, buddy." He snatched the doorknob. "I won't fail. You have my word on it."

Jordan clamped his teeth. A month ahead of schedule? Damn, nothing was going right. He reached into his in box while picking up the phone to call the marketing department. "Good afternoon, Chad. This is Jordan."

"Hello, boss," said Chad in his gravelly voice.

"I didn't receive your department's progress reports this morning. Is there a problem?" Jordan's gaze centered on a pink voucher.

"No, sir. Everything is on schedule. The reports will be on your desk in a few minutes. The courier has already been by to pick them up."

He nodded against the phone as he read the voucher. "Twelve hundred dollars from Barrette's Floral Shop?"

"Excuse me, sir?"

Jordan's eyes widened in alarm. "Nothing. I'll call you back after I receive your report. Bye." He hung up and pushed the intercom for his secretary. "Charlotte, can you come in here for a moment?"

She appeared immediately. "Yes?"

"This voucher?"

Charlotte slapped her hands against her hips. "What now? Let me guess. I ordered the wrong colors? Or perhaps the violinist was lousy?" she suggested sarcastically.

The dinner! Jordan felt sick. That was a week ago. How in the hell had he forgotten about the romantic dinner he'd planned? "No. That'll be all. Thank you."

She shrugged, then left the office.

He grabbed the phone. *I don't believe this.*

"Boss, we have a problem." Eric Graham rushed into his office.

Charlotte followed behind him. "He insisted on seeing you."

Jordan hung up. "What is it?"

"Our main distributor in New York has terminated their contract with us."

"Get me Cornell on the phone," he ordered Charlotte.

"Don't bother." Eric stopped her. "Cornell isn't taking our calls, either."

"What?" He returned his attention to his secretary. "Find copies of our contracts with Cornell."

"Yes, sir."

"Eric, I need you to update me on everything you know."

Moments later, Charlotte returned with a file. Jordan thumbed through it until he found what he needed. "We have it right here that ninety days written notice is required for cancellation. Charlotte, page the pilot. I want to be in New York in a few hours."

"Yes, sir."

Eric stood. "Should I tag along?"

"No, that won't be necessary." Jordan picked up the phone and called home to have an overnight bag packed.

The moment Jordan hung up, Charlotte returned. "You'll be ready for takeoff by two o'clock."

"Okay, that doesn't give me much time." He looked at his watch. "Call the limo driver. Also, get one of our marketing reps to find another distributor, just in case."

"Yes, sir."

Eric briefed Jordan on the situation, and by one o'clock Charlotte buzzed in to inform him that the limo had arrived.

Jordan packed his briefcase with the contents

of his in box and left his office, with Eric following close behind.

"Mr. Williams," Charlotte called after him.

Jordan turned as she raced to catch up with him.

"This just arrived for you. I had your bags rerouted to the plane."

"Thank you. Don't you think it's time you started calling me Jordan again?" he asked, accepting the envelope.

"I'm not so sure I'm ready to forgive you yet."

Jordan remembered Christian. "Damn."

Charlotte gave him a sharp look.

"Not you. I'll see you tomorrow."

"No, you won't. Tomorrow is Saturday, and you promised I could have at least one Saturday off this month."

He gave her his best puppy dog expression.

"No," she answered in a firm voice. "I'll see you on Monday." She turned and walked away.

He jumped into the limo and dialed Alex's apartment. Again, he was disappointed when he reached the answering machine. This time he left a message.

"Christian, this is Jordan. I'm so sorry about the dinner. Please let me make it up to you. We need to talk. I'm leaving for New York right now, but I'll be back in the morning. Let's meet at your favorite IHOP for breakfast, say ten o'clock? I'll—" The answering machine beeped and cut him off.

He slammed the phone down. Maybe he

needed to return later tonight instead. He had to do something. This nonsense had gone on for too long, and he wanted his wife back home.

He boarded the company plane and they lifted off on schedule. Once in the air, he reviewed a stack of contracts before remembering the envelope Charlotte handed him.

He opened it and pulled out a letter, scanned the contents, and stopped.

He read it again.

"I don't believe it. She actually filed for a divorce."

Eleven

A combination of stunned disbelief and anger boiled in Jordan's veins as he shot to his feet and stormed toward the cockpit.

The pilot looked up when Jordan entered.

"Turn this damn thing around."

"Sir, I can't do that. We—"

"You can, and you will."

"Our . . . our flight plans—"

"I'm not interested. You get whoever you have to on the radio, and you tell them we're heading back to Atlanta." Jordan stormed out. When he returned to his chair, he battled with his torrid emotions. *Damn. How could I have been so stupid?* The gravity of his actions in the past week filtered into his troubled thoughts. He groaned, and wished he could turn back time. He'd really screwed up.

Impatient, he grabbed the phone and dialed Alex's apartment number from memory. He reached the answering machine and slammed the phone down. "Where in the hell is she?"

He thought for a moment. Malcolm!

Despite his belief in their innocence, Jordan called his brother's office.

He reached his voice mail.

Suspicion clouded his mind as unlikely scenarios played in his head, no matter how hard he tried to ignore them. "Calm down," he recited to himself, but that was easier said than done.

He looked out the window. *Why in the hell is it taking so long to turn around?*

Christian polished off the last scoop of ice cream, then plopped back against the couch, stuffed. This was crazy. At this rate, a larger size wardrobe seemed inevitable. She looked at the phone and wondered who had hung up before she'd been able to answer. Well, maybe they'd call back.

Placing the laptop on her legs, she stared at the blank screen. She needed to complete her column by morning, which would take a miracle at this rate. She thought of calling Alex, but they'd had their fair share of pity parties lately.

She leaned forward and picked up her airline ticket. A trip home was just what she needed. With her marriage in ruins, she wanted to run home with her tail tucked between her legs. It wasn't fair, but a broken heart is what she got for believing in fairy tales.

Her mind traveled to Jordan. Where was he? What was he doing? She took a deep breath. Had he received the divorce papers?

She shook her head in disappointment, disgusted for harboring hope. It didn't make sense, but nothing made sense any more. Tired, she closed the laptop and put it away. Maybe if she lay down for a few minutes, she would rejuvenate. Inside the guest room, she plopped heavily onto the bed and closed her eyes to allow her mind to transport back to happier times. . . .

Christian shrieked with excitement while she remained cradled in Jordan's arms as he kicked open the door to their honeymoon cabin. Her eyes widened at the sight of its timeless beauty.

"Oh, Jordan," she whispered.

"Do you like it?" He lowered her to her feet.

She moved farther into the room, her eyes dancing off precious western antiques that gave it authenticity. "It's perfect." With a bright smile, she raced back into his arms and kissed him soundly on the lips.

Jordan laughed. "That's what I was aiming for—perfection." He disappeared to retrieve their luggage, while her attention returned to exploring. She remained amazed by the great detail that had gone into the place.

"Uncle Charles was a great lover of American history," Jordan said as he reentered the cabin. "I knew you'd appreciate his efforts."

"If Bobby saw this place, she'd swear that she'd died and gone to heaven." Christian stood admiring a painting when Jordan enclosed her in his arms. "Did your uncle paint this?"

"Quite an artist, huh? He depicted this from other pictures and came up with this."

"He's very talented."

Jordan snuggled kisses along her neck, causing her to wiggle playfully.

"So, Mrs. Williams, what shall we do first?" he whispered against her ear.

"Hmm. Mrs. Williams. I like the sound of that." She turned and met his lips in a hungry kiss. Her heart melted as she leaned against him.

His lips scorched a path from her mouth to reside at the hollow base of her neck.

Her soft moans of pleasure filled the room.

But as suddenly as their passion began, it cooled.

He pulled back and gazed at her through lowered lashes. "Should we move this to a . . . a more comfortable spot." His eyebrows jiggled mockingly for emphasis.

She smiled saucily, then turned toward the kitchen. "You know, I think I'd rather get something to eat. I'm famished."

He grabbed her hand and pulled her back against him. "I'm hungry, too, but not for food." He kissed the tip of her earlobe.

Christian hunched up her shoulders, trying to prevent his mustache from tickling her ear. "I'll tell you what." She turned and shared a quick kiss. "Why don't you fix something to eat while I slip into something more . . . comfortable?"

He lifted an interested brow. "Now that sounds more like it." He kissed her again.

She quickly retrieved one of her bags and disappeared into the single bedroom. When she closed the door and faced a large mahogany bed, her heart stopped.

Magnificent, she thought.

As she moved closer, her gaze roamed over the pearl-colored linen. Instant fantasies of what she and Jordan would do floated in her mind. Another smile caressed her lips.

Christian rushed to run her bath. She welcomed the water's warmth as she bathed with her signature jasmine-scented soap. She carefully dressed in a sheer lavender gown, then stared at her reflection in the mirror.

She hadn't gotten used to the breast implant, but in a way, it made her feel provocative—sexy. She smiled and winked at her reflection before rejoining her husband.

Jordan lit the fireplace. "Seems we made it in before the rain started," he said with his back to her. He stood and faced her. Delight sparkled in his eyes.

Christian's cheeks warmed as she twirled around to show off her sheer gown. The fire served as the only light, and its luminous glow gave Jordan a clear view of what awaited him.

"Now I think I've died and gone to heaven," he announced as he moved closer to embrace his new bride.

A thunderclap caused Christian to jump. Rain pounded on the windows.

Aware of her fear of storms, he took her hands. "Don't worry. Everything's going to be all right." He led her to a rug placed in front of the sparkling flames of the fireplace.

A small tray of assorted fruit sat in the middle of the rug while two glasses of wine shimmered beside it.

Her heart raced. *I've married the most romantic man.* When she looked back at him, he'd removed his shirt, and she stared wantonly at his muscular chest.

They kneeled down together.

Jordan picked up a plump strawberry, then leaned forward to tease her lips with it.

Playfully, she tried to bite into the succulent fruit, but he pulled it away each time before she could catch it. By the time she did, she had developed a severe case of the giggles.

"Mrs. Jordan Williams, how did I finally get you to the altar?" He spoke with a note of wonder in his voice.

She took a sip of her wine, then gave him a seductive smile, "The point is that you did."

He hesitated. "My mother—"

Christian placed her finger against his lips. Of course, it did hurt that her mother-in-law had refused to attend their wedding, but she didn't want to discuss it, not now. "Let's just talk about us tonight."

Jordan kissed her strawberry-flavored lips as

she ran her hand over the length of his shoulders.

When his tongue slid between her parted lips, she trembled, then sighed as he brushed his lips lower to the scented hollow of her throat.

Her head tilted back while she rode a wave of sensations. As his hands moved to tease her right breast through her gown, her nipple tightened beneath his toying fingers.

Brushing the fruit tray aside, he focused his attention on her. He slid the straps of her gown down to reveal her smooth dark skin.

Her crescent-shaped eyes caught a glimpse of her husband's passion-filled ones. *Breathtaking,* was the only word that came to mind.

His head descended, and with his tongue he encircled her trembling nipples.

Trees rustled outside the small cabin, and the melodious rain was like sweet music against the windowpanes.

Jordan pulled her gown over her hips, then down her legs. When she lay nude beneath him, he picked up the thin wineglass and spilled its contents over her breasts. Lowering himself, he feasted, teased, and plunged his tongue over every inch until he'd licked them clean.

He sought her lips again.

She fumbled with his pants, then removed them so that nothing existed between them. She felt wanton, brazen, and wicked even as she arched her body against him.

"Is the student trying to teach the teacher?" Jordan asked huskily.

Christian blushed.

"Let's just take our time," he whispered, then disappeared to trail kisses down her chest, her navel, and—

His first kiss of her darkened haven caused her eyes to widen, and her legs to instinctively close. "Jordan—"

"Shh. Open for me, baby," he coaxed with his seductive voice and hot hands.

When he leaned over her again, his artistry was so delicate, his expertise so masterful, that she lost herself in the rapture. Wild sensations swirled and pulled at her soul.

Tears of pleasure slid from her eyes. "I want to touch you, too," she begged.

"Ah, eager," Jordan teased, rolling onto his back.

She reached and cupped him with her hands, and felt his need pulsate against her palm. She slid her hand up and down his erection while marveling at how something so hard could feel so soft.

Breathless, he covered her hand and intimately guided her into a slow, yet effective rhythm. His eyes drifted closed as he fought his explosion.

"Did I do something wrong?" she asked through a haze of desire. She could feel him throbbing like a heartbeat within the circle of her hand.

Gently, he pushed her back onto the rug. "No,

Mrs. Williams. You're doing everything just right." He placed his hands between her legs and murmured, "You're ready for me." It was a statement, not a question, yet she nodded in response, anyway.

She was tight, but Jordan's penetration was gentle. She tensed, but soon his soothing rhythm intensified. Pleasure-filled cries blended with the rain's music to perform a beautiful duet.

Higher and higher she climbed as she rode the wave of a buffeting storm, her legs locked behind his thrusting hips. Her nails clawed against his back.

Jordan gripped her hips as his excitement heightened.

Her body exploded and slammed her with the force of a thunderclap, and her world burst into an array of brilliant lights. . . .

Christian opened her eyes and crashed back to reality. Her pillow was soaked with tears and her soul ached as a result of the sweet memory. Could they ever return to the way they were?

Twelve

Moments after his plane landed, Jordan directed the limo driver to Alex's apartment. This time, while he warred with his emotions, anxiety jumbled his nerves into knots. How had he gotten to this point, where he didn't know how to talk to Christian? He shook his head.

"This can't be happening," he muttered under his breath. "Of course it's happening," he argued back. "What did you expect?"

He'd expected their marriage to last forever, and he'd expected his wife to stick by him through thick and thin. Now it seemed he'd expected too much.

When the limo rolled to a stop, Jordan bounded from the vehicle in one smooth stride. The night's icy winds sliced through his clothing, and yet, he wasn't cold. He was numb. He glanced up at the sky-rise apartments, drew in a deep breath and prepared for battle.

* * *

Christian woke at the sharp rap at the door. Surprised, she looked at the clock. Another knock drew her attention, and she jumped from the bed.

"Who is it?" she asked, approaching the door.

"Jordan!"

She stopped dead in her tracks as the air immediately dissipated.

After a brief pause, his voice thundered through the door. "Aren't you going to let me in?"

Forcing air into her lungs and one foot in front of the other, she managed to make it to the door. By the time she opened it, her heart seemed to have leaped into the center of her throat.

Jordan stood in the entryway, one arm pressed against the wall and the other jammed against his hip.

Christian shifted uncomfortably while her gaze roamed his physique. She fought the natural instinct to bury herself in his arms.

"Well, I guess it's a good sign that you didn't call security."

His venomous tone baited her anger, and she lifted her head in defiance to reply, "What a tempting idea." A cold shiver raced down her spine at his icy glare.

"It will take more than that to get rid of me." He pushed away from the door and entered the apartment. After a quick glance at their surroundings, he returned his attention to her. "Are we alone?"

"Unfortunately." She closed the door.

His expression hardened. "I didn't realize my presence upset you so much."

"Either that, or the lack of," she retaliated, surprised by her mounting fury.

"I can't believe you're this mad because I forgot our anniversary," he snapped and jabbed his fists at his sides. "I'm sorry. Is that what you want to hear?"

She reeled back as if slapped. "Is that what you think this is about—you forgetting our anniversary?"

"Then what the hell is this?" He reached into his jacket and withdrew the crumbled envelope.

She gave it a withering glance. "Can't you read?"

The ice had thawed, and in its place fire burned in the depths of his eyes. "It's a divorce notice."

Her gaze remained level with his. "I believe I notified you a week ago."

"Because of our anniversary?"

"Our forgotten anniversary was just the icing on the cake, Jordan." Frustrated, she tossed up her hands. "It's nothing and everything, all at the same time. You can't mean to tell me that you don't feel it, too."

"Feel what? You're talking in riddles."

"The emptiness in our—*marriage*, if you want to call it that. Hell, it seems as if there isn't enough room in your life for me *and* J.W. Enterprises."

"Please don't start that again," he warned, then turned to pace the floor. "You know how important the company is to me."

"I know all too well."

His features softened as he looked at her. "Why can't you understand? You run a successful business. I'd think that you, of all people, would understand what it takes."

"I still make time for us. Not that you'd notice."

"Would you rather have me fail so I could prove Noah right? Is that what you want—to be married to a failure?"

"Of course not." She turned defensive. "But what about us? What about all the things you promised?"

"You have the best of everything. What else could you possibly want?"

"*You*, damnit," she shouted. "I wanted *you*."

Her words lingered in the air as they fell into an awkward silence. Despite her efforts, tears streaked down her cheeks.

"Why did you come here?" Her voice was a whisper as she pushed a lock of hair behind her ear.

The mood shifted as Jordan's dark eyes centered on her face. "I had to try to fix this. I had to try to fix *us.*" Gone was his earlier hostility.

The words warmed her heart, despite the wall she'd built around it. His sudden vulnerability caught her off guard, and she almost preferred his anger. At the sight of longing in his eyes, she feared she'd lose herself in their intensity.

He closed the gap between them in two strides.

With no time for her to react, he encircled her in his arms. She looked at him.

"I can't give you a divorce. I don't believe it's too late for us."

She turned from his tight scrutiny, then tried to pull away, but couldn't. Their warmth easily penetrated her defenses. "Jordan—"

"Christian, hear me out."

"No." She recognized his opening to convince her that he'd change. "I don't want you to talk. I don't want you to fill my head with promises you can't keep." She found the strength to pull away. "You'll tell me you'll change, but we both know that you can't." She crossed her arms, hoping it would help stiffen her resolve.

"*We* can change." Jordan interrupted. He reached and clasped her hand in his own. "Or at least, find some type of compromise."

"I wish I could believe that," she said, shaking her head. "But how many times in the last few years have you apologized about forgetting one thing or another, then spent all of one day showering me with gifts as if that were some way to make up for it? I never wanted gifts. I wanted you."

"I'm right here," he declared, exasperated.

"But for how long?"

Jordan dropped his hands. "I won't be able to

bear it if you walk out on me, too." He referred to his father.

"I can't go on being second in your life. I won't sit by idly while you're out trying to conquer the world."

"I always thought that *we* were trying to conquer it together." He lowered his gaze. Her speech had knocked the wind from his sails, but he searched for the right words to convince her of his sincerity.

She pressed her lips together and blinked her eyes dry. "I refuse to live this way. I deserve better."

"Chris—"

She placed a silencing finger against his mouth. She needed to finish. If there was a chance for them, then she needed to make him see how abandoned she'd felt. "Your company has practically been the air you breathe. There isn't any room left for us."

"Have I hurt you so much that you could actually turn your back on our marriage?" He searched her face. When she didn't respond, he closed his eyes. "I see."

Christian bit her lower lip to prevent it from trembling. "I don't know what you want me to say." She pulled her hand from his grasp and walked to the windows. She stared out at the view through a thin sheen of tears. The seductive scent of Jordan's cologne told her that he now stood behind her. She braced herself and prevented her tears from falling.

"I can't lose you." Jordan touched her shoulders.

The misery in his voice tore at her heart as a knot enlarged in her throat. She turned, and his lips landed hard against hers in a deep, demanding kiss. His dark, rich taste seeped into her mouth, into her blood, causing it to burn. When he caught her lower lip between his teeth, her resultant shudder sent thousands of tingling sensations throughout her body. Her head filled with the sounds of a roaring hurricane, and her body burned as bright as the sun itself.

Jordan ran his hands along her smooth curves and taut muscles with a suave, practiced touch that quickened her breath and elicited a murmur of pleasure.

He pulled her closer and dragged his mouth down to her throat.

Though she was caught up in their private world, small bits of reality pried their way into Christian's blurry thoughts. She gingerly opened her eyes. It took all of her strength to pull away.

"This isn't right," she managed to gasp.

"Of course, it is. We're married. We belong together," Jordan moaned. His hands moved and became entangled in her hair as he leaned down to capture another kiss.

She shook her head. "No. We can't do this." She moved away and straightened. Her heart screamed, but she ignored its longing.

"Chris, please," he muttered.

She took a deep breath, then answered, "I

need time." She watched his face cloud in disappointment "*We* need time." She moved closer
and looked directly into his eyes. "When I first
came here, I just wanted proof that I meant
something in your life."

"You mean the world to me. Why can't you
see that?" His hands framed her face. Love
shone in his eyes, making it harder for her to
continue.

"After this past week, I've realized we have so
many problems. There's even a question of trust
lingering between us. The accusations you hurled
at Mick's were unfounded."

Jordan dropped his hands only to shove them
into his pockets. "I'm sorry about what happened the other day. There's no excuse for what
I did. I know there's nothing between you and
my brother."

"But you *did* believe it. For that one embar-
rassing moment you believed it. Do you know
how that makes me feel?" Her anger returned.

"I'm sorry. If I could somehow erase that day
I would. I was hurt. And seeing you two together . . . I was jealous. As I said, I couldn't
remember the last time I saw you laugh and
smile that way with me, and it tore me apart."

She walked over to the couch and sat down.
Resting her elbows against her knees, she held
her head in her palms. "You said some ugly
things that I've forgiven. It's just that I can't forget. And it makes me wonder—what happened
to us?"

"Sweetheart, come home." He lowered to one knee—his pride be damned.

She met his gaze. Her breathing became labored, while her heart seemed to reside in her throat. "I can't." She choked out her answer.

He closed his eyes. "I understand."

"No, you don't."

He glanced back at her glossy eyes. "I'm trying to. God knows I am."

"At least that's a start." She prayed for courage. His melancholy expression intensified her pain. Yet, somewhere deep inside she knew she was doing the right thing. She had to be strong. She owed that much to herself.

"Maybe I should go now." Jordan stood.

She got up and nodded just as a tear managed to escape and roll down her cheek. Before she could react, Jordan gently wiped its tracks, and in its place gave her cheek a quick kiss.

"Good night." He turned and headed for the door.

Christian listened to his footsteps as she followed him, wishing there were something she could say, but she couldn't think of anything. Her eyes remained glued to the broad span of his back.

Jordan stopped and faced her again. "I understand that you need time, and I believe wholeheartedly that we can work this out. I still mean what I said earlier—I won't give you a divorce."

Thirteen

Alex strolled along Pier 39 and casually observed the mill of activity around her. She breathed in the various aromas drifting from cafes and restaurants as she passed. A breeze, chilled by the surrounding ocean, ruffled her dress and caused her hair to billow behind her.

The solitude gave her a chance to clear her troubled thoughts. She stopped at a railing and stared out at the Golden Gate Bridge. The day seemed perfect, the view breathtaking. She wished time could stop and allow her to bask in the day's beautiful weather.

"I was glad to get your call," Robert said in his deep, resonant voice from behind her.

Alex closed her eyes and drew in a long breath, but refused to turn around. "Thank you for meeting me here." She barely heard her own voice above the increasing winds.

"Believe me, I was happy to come." He placed his hands on her shoulders and proceeded to give her a light massage. I've missed you the last couple of days."

She shrugged off his hands and stepped away. "This isn't easy for me." She faced him.

Dressed in casual jeans and a white shirt which complemented his midnight complexion by bringing attention to the contrast of colors, he was definitely a handsome man. The problem was, he knew it.

His confident smile faded. "Don't tell me you dragged me down here for another tongue-lashing." When she didn't respond, he tossed up his hands in defeat. "Why can't you just let this go? You're worse than a broken record. I know what I did was wrong. How many times are you going to make me apologize?"

Alex struggled to control her temper. "I'm not here to wrestle another apology from you." As she met his dark eyes, an ache of regret gripped her.

"Then you came here to forgive me?" His smile broadened as he moved closer.

"No."

His shoulders sagged. "Then why in the hell did you bring me out here?" He shifted gears. "No chance of us having a quickie for old times sake?"

What in heaven's name had she ever seen in this man? "Robert, please." She closed her eyes, feeling her control slipping. "Just hear me out."

He stepped back. "What is it?"

Just say it. She met his gaze. "I'm pregnant."

Robert's handsome features crumbled as his eyes widened with disbelief.

Alex sucked in a deep breath. The air had thinned.

He blinked, seemingly unable to speak. The strained silence became unbearable.

"Say something before I start worrying whether our child will inherit that dumb look on your face."

"It's not mine." Robert voiced his denial in a mumbled rush. "It can't be."

She felt sick. "You *are* dumb, aren't you?"

He blinked again, then ran both hands along the sides of his short-cropped hair. "W-well, what are you going to do? Do you need money or—"

"Stop right there." Alex's temper won the war. "First of all, the last thing I need from you is money. I'm only telling you about this because I'm going to have your child, and it will need a father."

"What? Are you crazy? You can't have that baby. My wife will divorce me if she ever finds out."

Alex received the hard blow with an uplifted chin. "And we can't have that, now can we?"

Robert moved forward and gripped her shoulders. "You don't understand. She'll cut me off. I wouldn't get a dime, because I signed a damn prenuptial agreement."

Her eyes narrowed. Had she seriously believed she cared for this man? "Let go of me, and get ahold of yourself," she demanded.

He released her, then managed to say, "I'm sorry."

"Yeah. You are." Alex replied and walked away.

"Wait." He raced after her. "What are you planning on doing?" A wild look of desperation filled his eyes.

"I've already told you. I'm having a baby. It's up to you whether you want to be a part of its life. I've fulfilled my obligation by telling you about it."

"Alex, I need you to calm down and really think about this. I know you're angry at me, and maybe you're having this kid just to get back at me or something. But this is going to extremes. I know you. You won't be able to handle the life of being a single mother. What about your career? You're thirty-six years old. If you stop to have a baby now—"

"What? Don't tell me you're going to try to convince me that my career will be over just because I stopped to have a child?"

"Come on. We both know the life span of a model isn't long."

"Go to hell." She pushed past him.

He grabbed her arm. "Wait. I'm sorry. I didn't mean to go there."

"Look." Her patience hung on by a thread. "I'm not going to beg you to be a man. We'll be just fine. If you want out, I'm offering you the door."

Robert stood erect.

"But I'm warning you, if you walk out there's no coming back." Alex watched as her meaning sank in.

They stood staring at each other for a long painful moment.

His eyes glossed over as he shook his head. "I'm sorry, but I can't do this with you," he finally answered.

A strange combination of relief and disappointment warred within her. "I'm sorry, too." She forced a smile, then walked away.

As she continued to stroll along the pier, she allowed the cool air to kiss and brush away her tears.

Malcolm tapped his golden pen against the conference table while listening to the new campaign pitch from the marketing department. His expression remained stern, but he couldn't miss the loud grumbles Noah made at the head of the table.

The presentation ended, and the room fell silent. The men waited for some response from their employers, shifting uncomfortably in their chairs. Finally, Malcolm removed his reading glasses and pinched the bridge of his nose.

"Thank you for your efforts," he began. "But we need something that says *class*." He ignored the risqué pictures posted around the room.

"We were under the impression that you wanted a modern approach," said Bill Braxton from the marketing group.

"Modern, yes, but with a little more taste." Malcolm watched as Bill's face tightened from the insult. He glanced at his father, whose expression shouted, 'I told you so.'

"What my son is trying to say is thanks, but no thanks." Noah leaned forward in his chair, something he always did when he grew serious. "If this is the best our department can do, we'll have to go with an outside agency." He didn't wait for anyone to respond before he bolted out of his chair and left the conference room with angry strides.

Malcolm snapped the promotional layout closed and tossed it to the middle of the table. His shoulders slumped as he leaned back in his chair. He was disgusted by what had been presented.

"We can go back to the drawing board with this," Bill offered. "I know we can give you what you want."

Wanting to be a bridge over troubled waters, Malcolm felt torn. Maybe his father had the right idea. If they wanted to do something fresh and different, perhaps they needed to find it outside. He looked back to Bill and shook his head. "I think he may have a point on this one, guys."

There was low murmur from the men, and Bill seemed to look at him with desperation. There were no words exchanged, and the men quickly cleared the table.

Malcolm remained in his chair long after the last man left the conference room. At least Noah hadn't tossed the whole idea of changing their image out the window. But Malcolm knew he was treading on thin ice. A few agencies he respected came to mind. The test was convincing his father to meet with them.

Grabbing the briefcase, he gathered his things and left the room. His first stop was his father's office.

"Come in," Noah shouted through the door.

Malcolm entered the room, shaking his head at his father, who tried to hide a drink. "You know better than that," he warned as one would a child.

"Spare me." Noah's drink resurfaced.

Malcolm joined him at the bar and poured himself one. "That wasn't what I had in mind for Opulence."

Noah drained his glass before he answered with a tinge of bitterness in his voice. "Lately, I don't know what you have planned."

Malcolm frowned. "What do you mean?"

"Just what I said. You move through this place as if I don't exist. You make conferences without informing me. You make plans that I'm usually the last to know about." He poured another drink.

Malcolm covered the drink with his hand. "I think you've had enough."

"Damn it. I'm the president of this damn company and I'm your father. If I want a drink, I'll damn well have one!"

Malcolm flinched from Noah's hostility. "I didn't know that you felt this way."

Noah grunted and set his drink down heavily,

splashing most of its contents onto the bar's surface. There, just as quickly, his anger dissolved. His face became that of a man defeated. He squeezed his eyes shut and exhaled.

Malcolm set his own drink aside and slapped a hand against his father's shoulder. "Why don't you tell me what's really on your mind?"

Noah briefly locked gazes with his son before turning away. "The problem is I'm not getting any younger." He moved over to his desk. "I remember running through these offices with as much vigor and eagerness as you. My co-workers respected my views, and my determination to take Opulence into a new direction."

Malcolm watched the variety of emotions displayed across his father's features and began to understand.

"I've worked here for over fifty years, and maybe it's time I passed the torch."

"Why? You're doing a great job."

Noah laughed and shook his head. "I can see what's happening around here. You're a great leader, and Opulence needs you. My days here are numbered, and I'm having one hell of a time facing it."

Malcolm felt uneasy with this conversation. Opulence meant the world to his father. "Dad, I've told you before that the only reason I try so hard is because I know how much you really wanted Jordan here to run the company. I want to prove to you that I'm just as capable. I know I wasn't interested initially, but things have changed. I don't want to run it *for* you, but *with* you."

A small beacon of light flared in his father's eyes. "Do you mean it?"

Malcolm broke into a wide grin. "Of course."

"Good." Noah's chest expanded with pride. "First, I think you need to get a better handle on this so-called fresh campaign."

Malcolm saluted his father. "Yes, sir." He turned and headed for the door, but before he slipped out he faced his father. "And by the way, Mr. President, I still suggest you lighten up on the drinking or I'll call Mom."

Fourteen

Jordan hated this waiting game with Christian. He wanted his wife home. No longer did he feel cocky about her quick return, or his ability to smooth things over. In fact, he felt downright worried about losing everything.

His muscles strained as he struggled to make the last bench press. Sweat blanketed his body while a low growl rumbled from his chest. His arms trembled beneath the heavy weights, but his determination to complete the rep prevailed.

Clarence appeared and helped ease the bar back into the cradle above Jordan's head.

"An interesting method of suicide, if you don't mind me saying so," he said with his usual sarcastic wit.

"I mind." Jordan sat up. "But thanks, anyway."

The older man smiled. "A bonus would be the perfect way to show your gratitude."

"I'm sure it would be." He returned the smile and grabbed a nearby towel.

"Your mother is here to see you."

Groaning, Jordan draped the towel around his neck. "This early?"

Clarence shrugged, but concern etched his features. "She does appear to be upset."

"What's new?" He stood and reached for the water bottle. His mother's flare for dramatics was the last thing he needed.

"Should I tell her you're detained?"

"Of course not." He headed for the door. "She'd comb this entire house, then skin my hide for trying to avoid her."

Clarence laughed at the truth in his words.

Moments later, Jordan found Rosa in his office, hovering over the desk. His gaze fell to the divorce notice laying a few inches from where she stood.

"Well, good morning." Sunshine seemed to pour from her smile.

He concluded instantly that she'd read the notice. "Morning."

They crossed the room and exchanged hugs.

After a strange period of silence, Jordan inquired, "So what brings you here so early?"

"Your father."

His brows furrowed at her matter-of-fact reply. "Is that so?"

"Of course Noah doesn't know that I'm here. But I made a decision, and since neither of you are man enough to try to put the past behind you, it's up to me to correct the situation."

"I'm not interested."

Rosa continued as if she hadn't heard him. "Since you will apparently have more time on your hands, I figure that a nice dinner will be the perfect solution. Let's say around seven-thirty?"

"No."

Her cheeks brightened. "I'm not asking this time." She met his heated gaze with one of her own. "You can either do this tonight or tomorrow. I don't care which."

Surprised by his mother's change of tactics, he struggled to back out of the corner she'd forced him into. "I don't mean to be disrespectful, Mom, but this really doesn't concern you."

She squared her shoulders as if preparing for battle. "You know, I'm amazed that two men who haven't spoken to each other in fifteen years can be so damn much alike." She pressed her index finger against the center of his chest. "Is your pride worth so much that you'd sacrifice your family?"

"He disowned me, remember?"

"So, two wrongs make a right?"

"No, but it makes it even." Jordan shook his head and moved past her. "I don't want to discuss this any further. If he wants to see me, he knows how to contact me."

"Trust me. He regrets this whole mess, but is too damn stubborn to do anything about it." She walked over to stand in front of her son. "Just answer me this. Is continuing this nonsense worth all this pain and anguish?"

When he didn't answer, she proceeded. "I know he's hurt you. Sometimes we hurt the ones closest to us, but it doesn't mean that we stop loving them. And your father has never stopped loving you."

Jordan tensed.

Rosa laid a reassuring hand against his arm. "Please. Do this for me."

Pulling his gaze away, he struggled to do the right thing. "I can't."

She lowered her hand. "I'm sorry to hear that." She turned and headed for the door, but stopped before opening it. "I'm also sorry that I won't be able to see you anymore."

Jordan jerked around and stared incredulously at her.

She faced him. "Your parents are a package deal. This crazy situation is destroying me, and neither of you seem to give a damn." She lifted her head. "The choice is up to you."

Without another word, she left the office.

Clarence met her outside the door.

"So how did I do?" she asked as he escorted her to the front door.

"An Academy Award performance, ma'am." He winked.

"Do you think he'll show up?"

"I don't think he's the one we should be worried about."

"You leave Noah up to me." A confident smile appeared. "I'll get him there."

* * *

"Hello?"

"Is it done?" an impatient voice rasped through the line.

Elliott's hand covered the phone as he looked around.

"Is it done?" Emphasis was placed on each word.

He hesitated, then replied with dread, "Not yet."

"What in the hell do I pay you for?" The angry retort hissed through the phone. "Need I remind you what's at stake here?"

"Of course not," he snapped. "This isn't an easy job."

"That's not my concern. You were paid good money for the job, and you assured me you could do it."

"There are certain risks involved," he interrupted.

"I don't give a damn about the risks."

The line went silent.

"I'll finish the job, but I need a little more time," Elliott insisted. In the back of his mind, he wondered just how he was going to complete this assignment.

"When will I hear from you?"

A headache throbbed in his temples. "I can't give you a definite answer right now, but you'll be hearing from me soon. I can promise you that."

"Promises are comforts for fools."

Elliott wiped the thin sheen of sweet from his brow as he again looked around to be sure that he was alone. "I need at least four more days."

A soft strum of static crackled over the line.

"You have until four o'clock today."

"Four?"

"And don't be late."

Fear lumped in his throat. "You don't have to worry. I will make sure that J.W. Enterprises' software doesn't get off the ground."

The line went dead.

Christian and her assistant studied the potential layouts for magazine covers.

"It's all wrong," she said, shaking her head. She caught Mandy's sigh of frustration, and looked up. "This isn't what we discussed last week."

Mandy, a rich, ebony-skinned beauty with dyed platinum blond locks, stood just over five feet. She struggled to hide her irritation. "This *is* what you chose last week. You've changed your mind about this cover a dozen times. I'm beginning to think you don't know what you want."

Christian arched her brow. "I know perfectly well what I want."

Eyes wide with contrition, Mandy tried another approach. "I only meant that—"

"Our costs have now doubled because we have to start over. And it will be done as I instructed."

"Yes, ma'am," Mandy replied, despite a flash of irritation. Tension layered the room while she gathered the photographs.

Christian massaged her temples, troubled by her own behavior. She was being hard on her employees, but damn if she could help it.

She turned as Mandy reached for the door. "I didn't mean to blow up at you. The photos were nice. But I still want to go with the other plans."

Mandy faced her. The moment their eyes met, her expression softened. "It's okay. I'll get these changed right away."

When the young woman left her office, Christian exhaled a rush of air from her lungs. She needed to get a grip, and fast. No doubt Jordan had gone to work today and acted as if everything were normal, so she'd convinced herself she needed to do the same thing.

A quick knock sounded at her door a half-second before it swung open.

Malcolm poked his head around the door. Despite the quick recognition, her heart fluttered for a similar face.

"Do you mind if I come in?" he asked while entering anyway.

"Sure. I could use a break from the tough grind of publishing."

"I don't have a lot of time. I just wanted to swing by and see how you were doing."

She slid on a brave face and ignored her inner

turmoil. "Diagnosis—broken heart. Prognosis—I'll survive." She sat behind her desk.

"I'm happy to hear that." His smile brightened. "I would ask you to lunch, but after our last attempt—"

"I don't think that's a good idea." She laughed and held up her hands. "But thanks, anyway. I do have a few things I have to wrap up here before my flight tomorrow."

His brows heightened with curiosity. "Taking a business trip?"

"God forbid. Actually, I'm going home."

"Only for a visit, I hope."

"Of course. Just a visit." She strained to maintain her smile.

Malcolm nodded, then grew uncomfortable in the ensuing silence. "Well, I'd better go." He glanced at his watch. "I also have a plane to catch."

"Oh?"

"Yeah. Pop is unable to attend the jeweler's convention out in San Francisco, so I'm taking his place."

Her eyes widened, and a devilish gleam eased her smile. "Oh, really?"

"Yeah." His brows furrowed at her expression. "What's with the look?"

"Oh, nothing." She feigned ignorance, but couldn't erase the cat-with-a-secret look from her expression. "Just enjoy your trip."

He laughed, unsure of the joke or her sudden

mood swing. "Sure. I'll send you a postcard." He turned and whisked out of her office.

Christian crossed her arms and smiled at the closed door. "And say hi to Alex for me."

Fifteen

Alex removed her shades. Then, from behind the steering wheel, she stared at the brick building in front of her. Conflicting emotions swirled inside her, which didn't help her recurring nausea in the least. She didn't understand why she was there.

She cut the car's engine and leaned back. If she went through with this she'd never forgive herself.

Her heart muscles tightened. It wasn't fair; none of it seemed fair. This wasn't supposed to happen. She rolled her eyes to the heavens, searching for answers, for a sign—for anything, at this point.

The sky was so blue and the clouds were the whitest she'd ever seen. The view stole her breath. And for some strange reason, she couldn't pull her gaze away.

She didn't know how long she'd stayed that way, but her nausea had disappeared and a deep sense of calm replaced her torrid emotions. She reveled in this newfound sensation, and she trusted it.

Starting the car, she didn't know what tomorrow would bring, but for the first time since she'd learned of her pregnancy she believed that somehow everything would work out.

She shifted the gear into drive and pulled out of the parking lot of the abortion center.

Elliott lit his last cigarette. The pack had lasted less than an hour, which was how long he'd waited in this deserted alley. He hated this cloak and dagger crap.

"This is the last time I'm doing this," he mumbled, but his conscience quickly reminded him that he'd vowed that before. He shook his head. He needed to figure out a way to get out of this business.

As time ticked on and he took his last drag, he continued to badger himself about his actions. In truth, he respected Jordan Williams. He was a hardworking, self-driven man who knew what he wanted and worked to obtain it. Elliott admired the things he'd accomplished. He should be honored that a man of such caliber called him *friend*.

Since all of that was true, why was he here?

He discarded the cigarette butt and ground it into the concrete with the tip of his shoe as he struggled to keep his shame at bay. He took another glance at his watch: four-thirty. What was taking his contact so long?

It isn't too late to back out.

Elliott laughed at the thought. No telling what these people might do if he backed out now. He could lose everything, or spend the rest of his life behind bars. *But what you're doing could destroy J.W. Enterprises.*

"Damn it." He fished in his jacket for a new pack of Newports.

Heavy footsteps drew his attention to the alley entrance. His eyes grew wide with recognition as he gave an audible gasp.

"I figure I'd come down myself and meet you." Michael Andrew's smile grew wider.

"I should have known," Elliott whispered, stepping back.

Michael moved to a stack of crates leaning against a brick building and placed a black leather briefcase on it.

Elliott came forward. His curiosity got the best of him.

"As promised, I brought the other half of your money—upon delivery."

"Open it."

Michael's cool gaze met his. "Do you have my merchandise?"

"Of course." He reached for his own briefcase, at his feet. On the opposite end of the crates, he opened his case and displayed the contents.

With a mischievous and wicked gleam in his

eyes, Michael flicked open his case and showed the stacks of money inside.

The men cautiously exchanged sides to ogle their rewards.

Elliott snapped his case closed. "It's been a pleasure doing business with you."

Michael mimicked his actions. "Likewise." His gaze narrowed. "But I have to ask—what's your motivation for doing this? Aren't you and Jordy friends?"

Elliott patted his case. "This is all the motivation, and the only friend, I need."

It didn't take long for Rosa's plan to dissolve. As expected, Jordan contacted her and agreed to dinner. She regretted manipulating her son, but enough was enough. She, of course, had no intention of cutting ties with him, but what he didn't know wouldn't hurt him.

Noah was a different story. She'd left a dozen messages across the city for him, with no luck. At six o'clock, all she could hope for was that he'd arrive home for dinner at their usual time. She'd hoped to prepare him for Jordan's visit.

Clarence arrived to help her with her plan. Being that he was a longtime friend of the family, he also wanted to see this feud between father and son end.

Anxiety tied Jordan's stomach into knots during the drive to his parent's home. He practiced numerous speeches in the rearview mirror, but none set well with him. The thought of canceling crossed his mind, not that he actually believed his mother's threat to never see him again. She'd provided him with the perfect excuse to do what he'd lacked the courage to do for years.

Christian would be pleased, too, if in fact he and Noah were able to resolve their differences. It would also please him if his mother would make an effort to accept his wife. He shook his head at the impossibility of that notion. "This family is a regular soap opera," he muttered under his breath.

As he turned into his parents' estate an unexpected wave of mixed feelings assaulted his senses. Incredibly, at first glance at the house, the word 'home' echoed in his heart. He'd forgotten how much he missed the place.

His mother answered the door almost in the same instant he knocked. Her embrace was unusually tight, which filled him with the sense that he was doing the right thing.

"I'm so happy you came." She ushered him through the door.

"You didn't leave me with much of a choice," he answered as his gaze darted to his surroundings. There were a few new pieces of furniture, but overall the house still looked the same.

"Don't give me that." She playfully smacked his arm. "I know my men well enough to know that no one forces you into doing what you don't want to do."

Her comment won a smile from him. "And I

know you well enough to know that you were bluffing about never seeing me again."

"I plead the Fifth."

"I just bet you do."

"Well, your father should be along shortly. Can I get you something?"

Jordan glanced at his watch. He was a little early. "Sure. A Scotch on the rocks will be fine."

"I'll get that for you, ma'am," Clarence said, appearing out of nowhere.

"I should have known you had an accomplice." Jordan laughed.

Rosa smiled. "Come and join me in the parlor while we wait for your father."

The wait proved longer than she had anticipated. Seven-thirty turned to eight-thirty, then, soon, to after nine-thirty.

"I just don't know what happened." Rosa paced in front of the parlor window, occasionally glancing out of it.

"I do. He doesn't want to see me." Jordan stood, feeling like a fool for allowing himself to believe that his father truly wanted to end their feud.

"Jordan, please. I'm sure he'll be here any minute."

"Let's just face it. Noah has no intention of ever seeing me again. It's time we accepted that."

Rosa flinched from the pain she saw in her son's eyes. "Don't jump to any conclusions. I'm not sure he's even received my messages about dinner."

"I am." Jordan headed toward the door, with his mother fast on his heels. His entire body vibrated with anger and disgust. He had to get some air.

"Let's give him a few more minutes. I swear to you he couldn't have gotten my messages, or he'd have been here by now."

Jordan blocked out his mother's desperate plea. It was the only way to prevent himself from breaking down. "Good night, Mom." He kissed her cheek, then slipped out the door—heartbroken.

Sixteen

When Noah arrived home, well past midnight, it was as Rosa suspected. He'd never received a message informing him about dinner, but the excuse didn't protect him from the brunt of her anger. And for the first time in a long while, the couple went to bed angry.

Lying in bed, he stared up at the ceiling. His thoughts swirled in troubled confusion. It would be hours before the alarm clock sounded. And he doubted that he would have had a wink of sleep by then, either.

A tear escaped and formed a thin trail down his face.

Rosa's soft and steady breathing drew his attention. During the night, despite her earlier anger, she'd curled next to him with his right arm serving as an additional pillow. *Beautiful* was the only thought that came to mind.

For forty-three years his heart couldn't have been in better hands. Through every trial and tribulation, their love had grown stronger. He threaded his quivering fingers through her hair.

How he wished he could lie beside her for eternity.

His depression deepened.

Easing his arm from beneath her, he swung both legs over the side of the bed. The room tilted as a sudden wave of nausea propelled him to rush into the adjoining bathroom where, for the third time that night, he vomited.

Drained, he managed to drag over to the sink and splash his face with cold water. He relished the instant coolness against his hot skin and sighed with relief.

Looking up, he stared at his reflection in the mirror.

Time had been cruel.

His gaze traveled from the gray strands of his hair to the deep lines grooved into his skin. He was old.

A fresh wave of tears were held back by his returning strength. He pulled away from the mirror, and blotted his face dry. Moments later, he left the bathroom and crept out of the bedroom.

The house seemed unusually quiet, he noted, moving down the hallway. He dismissed the thought—of course the house would be quiet at three in the morning.

He traveled his usual path down the staircase, into the parlor, and over to the bar. Running his hands along the siding, he retrieved the key from Rosa's new hiding place and unlocked the cabinet. He needed a good stiff drink. No doubt it would settle his nerves so he could get some sleep.

At the first sip of Jack Daniels, his eyes drifted closed while he savored the taste. *Ah, just what the doctor ordered.*

Noah glanced down at his once trembling hands and saw they were as steady as a rock. He smiled.

Around the third or fourth drink, his thoughts once again became troubled. However, this time he didn't focus on his mortality, but on Jordan.

The alcohol hadn't helped his depression. Pride had caused this isolation from his son. And it was pride that still prevented him from picking up the phone. A sad laugh tumbled from him, and his shoulders slumped forward. Tears flowed from his eyes and continued to spill into his fifth and sixth drinks.

Much later, his mood shifted, and he made a desperate attempt to pull himself together. Maybe he *should* call. It was a silly thought, really—him calling Jordan. After so much time had passed, what would he say?

More importantly, what would Jordan say?

He shook his head. It didn't matter. There was no way he was going to grovel for forgiveness. After all, it was Jordan who had walked out on him.

Noah's hand trembled as he brought the glass to his lips. This time, he was unable to take another sip. He lowered the glass with a hard thump against the bar's surface. Some of its contents splashed over the rim.

Shame rode in like a tidal wave as he cupped his face in his hands and wept.

A few hours later, Rosa retrieved Noah from the parlor with the help of a servant and brought him up to bed.

Amarillo, Texas

The wide countryside of McKinley Ranch lay before Christian, welcoming her home. She shifted the rented Land Rover into gear and headed to the main house.

"Welcome home, Chrissy," Bobby boisterously greeted as she gathered her granddaughter into her arms.

"It's good to be home." She withdrew from Bobby only to fall into the arms of her Uncle Pete.

"We sure do miss you around here." He gave her a hearty squeeze before releasing her. When she pulled back, he took a good look while adjusting his Stetson hat. "Is everything awright?" he asked, concerned. "That city boy better be treating you right."

Christian summoned a reassuring smile. "Don't bother getting all worked up. I'm fine. I'm just here for a brief visit, that's all."

His frown deepened.

Dylan, her grandmother's husband, jumped in for his hug. "Glad to see you back home."

"It's great to see she hasn't run you off yet." She laughed.

"Not a chance."

"Come on, sweetheart." Bobby reached for her hand, rescuing her before Pete read the truth in her eyes. "I have your old room all ready for you."

The women slid their arms around each other as they entered the house.

Christian's spirits lifted the moment her gaze danced over the familiar decor. The instant she walked into her bedroom, time seemed to stop. "I hadn't realized how much I missed this place until now."

Her grandmother closed the door. "That's why you need to come home more often," she preached in her usual parental tone. Then her expression turned serious. "How are you holding up?"

No need for a façade, Christian knew. Bobby could always read her better than any book. "There are times when I think I'm doing just fine—like I can conquer the world. Then I wake up and realize I'm falling apart."

"Oh, sweetheart." Bobby closed the distance between them and enveloped her in her arms.

At the tender age of seven, life had dealt Christian a cruel hand. She'd lost her parents in a fatal car accident. She'd come to live with her grandmother then. And it was here, on this beautiful land, where she'd fantasized about raising her own family.

Then she met Jordan, and suddenly her old dreams were replaced with new ones. And her new home became wherever he was. Even now, that fact remained true.

She moved away.

"Have you told him you filed the divorce papers?"

"He received notice yesterday, and came by to see me last night."

Delight lit Bobby's eyes as she clapped her hands. "See. I just knew it. He might be stubborn, but he's no fool. I bet that notice knocked some sense into him."

She drew in a deep breath. "I don't know about knocking anything into him, but he made it clear that a divorce was out of the question."

"That's great news. Then everything is solved." One look at her granddaughter's somber expression and her excitement died. "Or maybe not."

Christian moved toward the window, the view already permanently etched in her memory. "It's not that simple. God, I wish it were." She gazed off into the distance and caught a glimpse of the secluded gazebo near the pond.

Scattered memories of the night that had changed her life flooded her mind. It was the first time Jordan confessed his love. She had held doubts even then. They were different people from different worlds. It almost seemed as if a cruel twist of fate had drawn them together. . . .

* * *

Jordan stood in the gazebo's arched entrance as her gaze traveled his length. He wore a pair of tight wranglers and a white, oversized shirt open to expose half of his chest. He was breathtaking.

"I thought you'd never get here," he said in a low, seductive voice.

Candles flickered behind him, and Christian shifted her gaze to an enticing candlelight dinner for two.

"What's this?"

Dimples grooved his cheeks as his slow smile weakened her knees. "It's dinner. I hope you're hungry."

Their eyes met.

"I thought you'd left," she whispered.

"Disappointed?"

Her mouth went dry as she shook her head.

"I'm glad to hear it." He stepped down and offered his hand to her. "Shall we?"

She accepted his hand while butterflies fluttered in the pit of her stomach. She stared down at the romantic setting with disbelieving eyes; it brought a subtle smile to her lips.

"I'm glad you like it," he said, pulling out a chair for her.

Christian sat. "It's beautiful."

"Just like you," Jordan whispered. He moved to the opposite side of the table and grabbed the bottle of champagne chilling in an ice bucket.

"May I ask why you went to all this trouble?"

"I would think that was obvious." His gaze caught and held hers prisoner.

The intensity of his gaze rendered her breathless. The sight of him wreaked havoc on her senses. *The magic won't last long*, she reminded herself. "I really appreciate what you're trying to do—"

"What am I trying to do?"

Speechless, she struggled for the right words. She had to stop this, stop where they were heading. "What I mean to say is—that *we* will never work."

Instead of getting angry, which she'd half-expected him to do, Jordan crossed his arms and leaned back in his chair to stare at her. "Are you about to give me your let's be friends routine now?"

She averted her eyes and swallowed the rest of her speech.

"I think you forgot that I've heard this one before. It was the night we met. Only then, you thought I was Malcolm." When she said nothing, he continued. "I believe the next phrase is something about you consider me to be more like a brother, and that you want us to remain friends. How am I doing so far?"

Christian shifted in her chair.

He reached across the table to take her hand in his. "I'll tell you what. Let's not think about anything past this moment—right here, right now. Let's just let tomorrow take care of itself."

A tempting offer, too tempting, but the voice

of reason shouted in her ears. She withdrew her hand. "You're making this difficult for me."

"Good. I intend to."

"Please don't do this," she whispered "There are some things you don't know about me."

"You mean about your breast cancer?"

Christian sucked in a sharp gasp of air. Her eyes stung with unshed tears. Silence stretched between them while she gathered her thoughts.

Jordan tried again. "I didn't mean be so blunt. I just wanted you to know that it doesn't matter to me."

"So you think you have me all figured out? Is that why you came here and staged this big production?" She jumped to her feet. Anger, rage, and a deep sense of shame washed over her in large tidal waves. "I have to go."

"Christian, wait." Jordan stood and cut off her path before she could step from the gazebo. "Please, just talk to me." The wounded look in her eyes pulled on his heartstrings. "I came here because . . . I love you."

A hysterical laugh stumbled from her lips as if he'd told a cruel joke. "Love me? Love me?"

A thin gloss shimmered in her eyes.

His hands ascended to touch her cheek. "Don't do this."

Christian recoiled from his touch. "So who told you?"

"Does it matter? Why didn't you tell me? I know you care for me. I can see it in your eyes. Why do you think it would matter to me—"

"Stop it!" she shouted, shaking her head to block his words. "You have no idea what it's like." Accusation trembled in her voice. "I wake up every morning and face . . ." She stopped and closed her eyes. "Do you know what it's like looking at my body in the mirror and not being able to feel whole? To wonder why this had to happen to me?" She faced him. "You can't possibly want me. You can't. I'm not whole. I'm not—"

Now infuriated, Jordan grabbed her shoulders. "Don't you ever talk like that."

She lifted her chin in defiance. "I've come to terms with my mastectomy. I have one breast, Jordan. That's my harsh reality. Can you deal with that?"

He searched her eyes. "If only you could see yourself through my eyes, you'd never ask me that." He lifted his hand and traced the delicate lines of her face. "Do you know what I see when I look at you?"

With her vision blurred, she shook her head.

"I see my life," he answered in a low voice. He moved closer, his head lowered, until their faces remained only inches apart. "I see everything that makes me complete. At this moment, I can't remember what I did or how I lived before you. But I do know that there is no way that I can go on without you. I can't leave here without you."

Her breath caught in her throat.

"You do believe me, don't you?"

Spellbound, she couldn't answer. She was afraid to, afraid that she would wake from a dream. She'd spent so much time pushing men away, afraid that once they'd learned about her breast cancer, learned that she wasn't what they wanted, they would reject her. And now, the man of her dreams had told her he couldn't live without her.

"You have to believe me," he whispered. "I want you to be a part of my life. I want you to be my wife."

Now, the memory faded as she stood, but an ache remained in Christian's heart.

Bobby moved and stood behind her. "Everything will work itself out in time. You'll see. Trust me. Things are simpler than they seem. And it seems to me that you're still very much in love with your husband."

Christian turned. "I'll never stop loving him."

Bobby pushed a lock of hair away from her granddaughter's eyes. "Then you're already halfway there in resolving the problem."

As she pressed her trembling lips together, Christian's confession escaped in a whisper. "But I'm so tired of being alone."

Bobby's instant embrace rewarded her with the comfort she'd come home to receive.

Seventeen

"What do you mean, she's gone?" Jordan tightened his grip on the phone.

"Calm down," Malcolm coaxed over the phone line. "She's just taking a brief trip home. I only called because I thought you should know. She said she needed time to think. You should understand that. I didn't want you to worry . . . or think that—since I'm leaving on a trip—that we've planned some secret rendezvous," he added with a laugh.

Regret filled him. "Mal, about the other day—"

"Forget it. At one time, I'd have reacted the same way."

"Thanks for understanding."

"But I'd suggest one thing—put your pride aside and go get your wife." His baritone deepened. "I've always regretted not going after Alex. I don't want you to go through that kind of pain."

Jordan's heart squeezed in response. "Thanks again, Bro," was all he could think to say before they ended the call. He placed the phone on the receiver and leaned back from his desk.

Over the years, he'd watched his brother try to cope with a broken heart. The day Alexandria walked out, Malcolm went from being the lovable jokester with a 'devil-may-care' attitude to a more grounded man who took responsibility seriously.

Jordan turned introspective. Life without Christian. His heart lurched at the mere thought. Had his visit last night scared her off? He tilted his head back against the chair and looped his wife's rings over the tips of his fingers.

He studied them for what seemed an eternity. He found comfort in a vision of placing the rings back on his wife's fingers, hoping that day would be soon. He hated their empty house even more now. He'd taken so much for granted. His roller coaster ride of emotions took a sudden dip, leaving his whole world somehow suspended in time.

The phone rang.

He grabbed it on the first ring. "Jordan Williams."

"I have some bad news," Quentin stated matter-of-factly.

Jordan groaned. "Now why doesn't that surprise me?"

"There's absolutely no way around this delay. We're going to need more time."

"Damn. Do you know what this means?"

"Yeah. It means that jerk at Compucom Systems stands a chance of beating us to the punch."

A large image of crow pie appeared in his mind. "All right. Schedule another meeting with the programmers. I want details as to where we are on this. We'll handle everything then."

He hung up.

Deflated, he glanced around his office, cursing at his luck. Then, he realized that he'd just allowed his work to distract him away from more important matters. And nothing was more important than Christian. He remembered vividly the night he'd discovered just that . . .

"Christian, let me in." He shouted from the opposite side of the door.

"Please, just go away," she begged in a hoarse whisper. The panic in her voice frustrated him.

"I'm not leaving until we finish what we started—what I started."

"You are finished. There can never be an us."

"Step away from the door and let me in."

Her silence was his answer.

"I'm going to count to three. If you don't move away from this door, I swear I'll cause a scene so loud it will wake the whole house. Is that what you want?"

"You wouldn't."

"One."

"Jordan, please listen to me—"

"Two."

"You will regret marrying me."

"Three!"

She stepped away from the door as he jerked it open and entered the bedroom.

Christian stood near the window, silhouetted by the moonlight. Jordan's gaze danced over her figure. His long strides swallowed the space between them.

When he stood only inches from her, he gazed down at her upturned face. Regardless of how much she tried to hide her emotions, he read them in the depths of her eyes.

They remained facing each other, neither uttering a word, each spellbound by the other's presence.

Jordan reached out and caressed her supple face. She lowered her head and closed her eyes.

"Look at me." He tilted her chin up. "Let me stay here with you tonight."

"I—I can't."

"Why?"

"I—I—"

"Don't you want me to stay?" He strode forward.

She stepped back.

He moved until her back pressed against the wall. "Say I can stay."

She shook her head.

"I want you," he murmured. "I've wanted you since the first moment I laid eyes on you." His head descended in an arc, capturing a kiss, seizing her breath.

She whimpered as his tongue darted boldly into her warm mouth, demanding more.

With her hands pressed against his chest, his hand descended.

She broke away. "Stop."

Short gasps of air heaved his chest, but he made no attempt to back away. "Do you really want me to stop?"

She didn't answer.

Their gazes locked as he cupped her face. "Please don't ask me to leave."

He settled his hand at the juncture of her neck and shoulder. His thumb dipped into the V above her collarbone. "Your pulse is racing."

She made a half attempt to pull away.

A low laugh rumbled from him. "You don't want me to go. Do you?"

She lifted her chin with tears shimmering in her eyes. "No." With that one word, she sealed her fate. The fear of rejection was mirrored in her eyes.

Jordan lowered his hand to the tiny buttons of her shirt.

Christian pressed her quivering lips together, stifling any further protest. Time suspended, hearts pounded, and love laced its invisible fingers between them.

Slowly, he slid her shirt over her shoulders. It fell and pooled around her legs. When she blinked, tears crested her lashes and trickled down her face.

"There's no need for these." He brushed a kiss along the dewy tracks.

"I'm scared," she admitted in a shaky whisper.

His lips lowered to settle against her mouth.

Her body arched. She draped her arms behind his neck and drew him closer.

He couldn't get enough of her hot, sensual mouth and tensing tongue.

Love. The word swirled inside his head as a warm glow radiated within him.

His hand curved around her waist. Their gentle rain of kisses soon turned into a raging storm of passion. Each sought what only the other could give.

Drunk from the sweetness of her mouth, Jordan felt a blistering heat rise and consume his soul. Her signature fragrance enchanted him as the softness of her body beguiled him. Hard with need and filled with longing, Jordan struggled with himself to prolong his seduction.

With a sense of urgency, Christian tugged on his shirt. His buttons opened with a snap. Her hands drifted up his bare chest, spreading the material of his shirt wide apart.

His hands lowered to cup her breast.

Christian stilled.

Jordan broke their kiss.

Against her will, tears slithered from her eyes, but she was unable to stop him, to stop the inevitable.

"Look at me." He coaxed. His fingers tilted her chin upward.

Swallowing, she lifted her shimmering gaze to his.

"Do you trust me?" he asked.

She opened her mouth, but no words came.

He waited.

Too scared to try speaking again, she nodded her response.

"Do you want me?"

She nodded again.

A smile raised the corners of his mouth as he unsnapped her bra.

She held her breath. It was the moment of truth. Fresh tears blurred her vision as she watched him while the material fell from her shoulders and joined her shirt puddled around her legs.

Jordan's head descended.

Christian's lungs threatened to burst.

When his lips made contact, a sweet world blossomed open at the feel of his soothing mouth pressed firmly against the thin scar along the flat surface of her left breast. She rolled her head back and flexed her fingers against the corded muscles in his back.

He remained positioned before her, raining kisses along her chest, before nestling his head so he could suck her right nipple. He pulled himself up, then forced her gaze to meet his. "You're beautiful."

Lips pursed, eyes shimmering, she felt love blossom within her.

Hope. She named the emotion. Hope for the chance of love, for the chance of the life she'd only lived in her dreams. She shook her head, not wanting to believe in the impossible.

Jordan lifted her as though she weighed nothing and carried her to the bed.

The mattress dipped as it supported their weight. She kissed him with blind need, seeking to fill the void she'd had in her heart for so long, too long.

His parted lips moved insistently against hers. She welcomed the suggestive evasion of his tongue, and matched his erotic rhythm with one of her own.

Jordan clenched her body tighter. His mouth dominated hers. The room tilted while her mind spun out of control. Wondrous sensations rippled through her body. Vaguely aware of the removal of her clothes, Christian arched her body beneath him.

Her movements became bold as she dipped her head to brush her lips across his chest. She relished the exquisite feel of his hard body.

His muscles flinched at her touch. His hands sank into the hair at her nape, then lifted her roughly to capture another hungry kiss.

Leaning over her, he kissed her senseless. She couldn't stand much more.

Jordan shifted for the top position, his hips insistent as his mouth skimmed along the lobe of her ear.

Her mind plummeted into a vortex of frenzied emotions. His legs wedged between hers, parting her thighs, and all the while his tongue tangled with hers. Suddenly, he stopped.

"Christian."

She surfaced from a haze, lifting her eyes to his. He cradled her face between his palms.

"Tell me what you want."

Stripped, vulnerable, and naked—she felt all those things, but she would die if he didn't continue this slow torture he'd started.

"I want you." Her confession hung in the air between them for a moment. She feared he would leave her wanting and needing him.

His hands glided down the contours of her body, stirring passion once again in their wake.

Christian sucked in her breath when his hand moved past the downy triangle between her legs, then dipped inside her slick passage.

She pressed her head back against the pillow. Every part of her body ached with longing.

His fingers went deeper, steadily increasing the tempo. She quivered beneath him. Passion mounted, then exploded into sparks of pleasure.

Christian fell limp beside him, too weak to move.

A rumble of laughter vibrated Jordan's chest. "Not yet, sweetheart. I'm not done with you."

Before she understood his intent, he lowered his head and settled against the gate of her passion. She reached to pull him up, but instead she threaded her fingers through the low crop of his hair, her hips arched to give his mouth better access. She couldn't think, let alone remember to breathe.

Cupping her bottom, Jordan feasted on her body's nectar. Her melodious moans hardened his masculine desire and drove him near the point of no return as he plunged onward. His name tore from her lips as an uncontrollable spasm shuddered throughout her body.

He ascended to her lips and fed her the taste of her body's honey. His hands caressed her chest, surprising her with the sensations that coursed through her left breast. With his body over her, she felt the pressure of his pulsating member rubbing against her wet entry. Anticipation rippled through her spent body.

Jordan's heart soared. He no longer resisted the sweet agony to unite their bodies. He called her name, straining with patience for her eyes to open.

"Christian," he coaxed.

She managed to open her heavy lids to meet his smoldering gaze. When she did, he penetrated her.

She gasped at his size as he filled her. Clutching his back, her fingers kneaded the taut, smooth skin. She marveled at his trim hips and firm, muscular buttocks.

Jordan set the pace with sleek, powerful strokes that teased and then fulfilled their promise of satisfaction. His body clamored for release, but he held a tight rein on his craving. He savored her body's sweetness as ragged gasps of air filled his lungs. He sank deeper into ecstasy.

He recited her name in a low, husky whisper as he moved his hands over the curves shaping her back. She clung to him. Heat deepened their insatiable hunger.

His mouth moved over the column of her neck to the base of her throat.

Pleasure rippled across her in the wake of his lips as he kissed her with excruciating and deliberate slowness. He etched her every curve in his memory, careful not to miss an inch. He wanted to remember her flavor, her scent, her cries of pleasure.

Christian's fingers clawed his back as she tightened around him.

Jordan's teeth clenched, and a deep groan rumbled from his chest.

Her nails sank into the groove of his back. Fireworks exploded behind the lids of her eyes, while a cry of fulfillment ripped through her.

Jordan savored each spasm of pleasure that poured from his weakened body. "I love you."

Waking from his memories of the past, Jordan jumped from his chair, grabbed his jacket then raced out the office. He was going to get his wife back.

Eighteen

Noah hated doctors. He'd never known them to say there was nothing wrong. They always found something to charge him for, even if it meant tripling the price of aspirins. He jumped when the stethoscope's cold metal touched his chest.

"Breathe in for me," Dr. Andrea Craig instructed. She was a young, dark-skinned beauty.

He wondered idly if she'd just graduated from medical school yesterday.

He complied, but not without rolling his eyes heavenward. He wished he hadn't indulged Rosa with this silly request. There wasn't anything wrong with him. All right, maybe he'd been drinking a bit lately, but he was allowed. He'd had a lot on his mind.

The doctor pressed the instrument in the center of his back. "Again."

For the next hour, he endured every test imaginable while thinking of a million things he'd rather be doing—like dancing naked in the middle of an ice storm.

"Have you experienced any strange symptoms lately?"

The question jarred him from a bored trance. Sure he had—nausea, vomiting, aching joints, and fever, to name a few. "Nah, I'm as healthy as a horse," he boasted.

Dr. Craig didn't respond, but her look suggested that she didn't believe him. She turned and wrote in his chart.

Noah changed the subject. "You know, I used to see your father. I hated it when he retired."

"I'm sure no more than he did," she returned his light banter. Then she became serious again. "Will you stretch out your arms and hold your hands steady for me?"

His brows heightened.

She looked up. "Please?"

Expelling a frustrated sigh, he held out his arms and saw with utter dismay how much his hands trembled.

She jotted something else down.

He lowered his arms. His witticisms eluded him.

"I want to schedule you for an EEG."

His eyes rounded. "What for?"

"I want to test for liver encephalopathy."

"And I want to meet the pope." Noah reached for his shirt. "I've had enough of these damn tests."

"Calm down, Mr. Williams." She spoke in a reassuring tone and smiled for the first time. "I can't help you unless I can run more tests."

"You just don't get it, lady." He held up his hand and counted off. "I've had an ultrasound, a computed tomography, X rays, and a damn liver biopsy. Enough is enough. If you can't find anything with those, then tough."

If his tone offended her, it didn't show. "There's no need to get hostile, Mr. Williams. I know that all of this seems a bit much, but it's the only way I can get some answers."

"Why don't you try asking me some questions?"

"Why? So you can tell me you're as healthy as a horse?" Dr. Craig's professional demeanor disappeared as she removed her glasses, crossed her arms, and looked him squarely in the eyes. "You know, I don't know whether you like lying to me, or to yourself. Now, if you'd like someone to pat you on the head and tell you whatever you'd like to hear, I think I may be able to refer you to another practice. On the other hand, if you want help, stay. But I'd prefer that you'd try to refrain from wasting my time."

Silence lapsed before a glint of admiration lit his eyes. "I see you've inherited your father's bedside manner."

"I should be so lucky," she replied with a slight smile, then reopened his chart. "Now, if you can be serious for a moment, I'd like to ask you a few questions." She stopped short before sliding on her glasses. "That's if you're going to be honest."

Noah nodded.

"Good. I see you were first diagnosed with liver cirrhosis about ten years ago." She looked up and made sure she held his gaze. "Are you still drinking?"

Rosa paced the floor. She'd waited for hours for Noah to return. Dread flowed through her veins. Convinced she'd die from worrying, despite forcing happy thoughts or struggling to find the silver lining around this dark cloud, she anticipated the worst.

She shook her head and damned Noah for being so hardheaded. Only a fool would believe his increased alcohol consumption hadn't led to further liver damage. She faced the well-stocked bar, suddenly filled with a desire to shatter every bottle.

Nothing she'd tried had convinced Noah to get rid of the alcohol. He'd always recited that he never knew when he needed to entertain guests, or that a successful businessman needed a stocked bar at all times. *Hogwash.*

Rosa's anger grew with each tick of the clock. Another hour passed. She called the doctor's office and reached a recording that stated the office had closed.

Submerged in troubled thoughts, she didn't hear the car pull up. But when the front door opened, Rosa raced from the parlor into the foyer. "What did the doctor say?" She stopped a few feet away from Noah.

He closed the door and with a lazy smile, he faced his wife. However, the sincerity missed his eyes.

"And don't tell me you're as healthy as a horse, either," she warned, crossing her arms.

His smile widened as he turned up the heat on his boyish charm. "Now, would I lie to my favorite girl?"

She warded off his attempt with expertise. "In a heartbeat."

"They just ran some tests. We'll know something within the next few days." He shrugged, then slid his hands into his pants pockets. "Satisfied?"

Rosa studied him for a moment, searching for the truth in his face rather than in his words. She knew his motivation would be to protect her, but in this case she'd rather face facts.

Trying to lighten the mood, Noah moved forward with outstretched arms. "Now, can I at least get some kind of affection from you, or are you planning to interrogate me for the rest of the night?"

"Don't tempt me."

A dramatic frown followed by his best woeful puppy dog expression was his next tactic. "Please?" he asked with his arms still spread wide.

She hated it when he did this. For a few seconds more, she pretended to remain indifferent to his charm, But she knew he wasn't buying her act when a glint finally lit his eyes. With a sly smile, she slid into his embrace.

The moment they embraced, a strange fear took hold of her, and she held on for dear life. Noah did the same.

Christian rode bareback across the land's green carpet on one of Uncle Pete's prized horses. The late afternoon's breeze threaded through her hair much like a lover's caress. Her troubled mind cleared, and her heart soared with freedom as she admired the surrounding beauty.

She rode for hours, drawing strength from everything she passed. Eventually, her problems galloped to the forefront. However, this time she sought possibilities of resolving or maybe compromising on many of the issues, as opposed to throwing in the towel.

"Relationships require compromise," Bobby had said over breakfast. Christian hated this seesaw of emotions. But her grandmother had been right about one thing—she was still very much in love with her husband. That fact alone kept a beacon of hope in her heart. Sure, Jordan was a stubborn workaholic. They were traits he'd received from his father, whether he wanted to admit it or not.

Christian laughed at the irony. Like father, like son. She pulled her horse to a stop. As she stared out at the breathtaking view of the sunset, she drew in a cleansing breath.

It was hours still before she returned to the house; in truth, she felt better than she had in years.

"I'm glad to see you remembered the way back home," Pete teased with a quick smile. He draped his arm around her shoulders and squeezed. "I thought for a moment there I was going to have to round up a posse to search for you."

An easy smile accompanied her soft laughter. "No need for all of that. I was just enjoying a relaxing ride." She eased an arm around his waist as they moved farther into the house.

"Is that husband of yours coming down any time soon? It's been so long since I've seen him, I'm beginning to forget what he looks like."

Christian kept her gaze averted. "Jordan is a little busy right now. I'm sure he'll want to come down and visit as soon as his schedule permits," she said, using a practiced speech.

"I know. I know. That damn company of his."

She stiffened.

Pete shook his head. "You know that's been his excuse for a while. It's starting to sound as if you married yourself a workaholic."

Christian's smile waned.

"Which means," he continued, "that city boy is neglecting my favorite niece."

"I'm your only niece."

"Don't get hung up on technicalities." He

stopped. His fingers lifted her chin in order for their eyes to meet. "I'm a great listener, and I have pretty broad shoulders. I mean, if there's a problem or anything."

Her entire being ached at the genuine concern laced in his eyes. She pushed up onto her toes and kissed his cheek. "Thanks. Of course I know you're always here for me, and I love you for it."

Pete lowered his gaze. "You know it's been years since Millie left me, and every day I think of something else I should have said to convince her to stay." The note of regret lingered between them.

"But you know," he added, "pride can be a man's worst enemy. And at one point in everyone's lives, we all learn that lesson the hard way. I just wish for me I had learned it sooner." His smile turned awkward before he left her alone to mull over what he had shared.

Pride was definitely another destructive trademark Jordan shared with his father.

She turned and went up to her room, determined not to make any rash decisions—like calling Jordan and taking him back. If she took him back now, she wouldn't have accomplished anything. The thought of returning to Atlanta saddened her.

Throughout the rest of the evening, Christian said little and thought plenty. She appreciated her family for not engaging her in many of their conversations. By the time dinner had ended, she excused herself and opted to take a walk.

Bobby escorted her to the door. "You make sure you're careful out there," she warned.

"I will." Christian kissed her cheek, then slid on a thin sweater and left the house.

She followed an old familiar path from the house and allowed the same questions to float through her head, questions she was no closer to answering. Her gaze darted around, filling her with a sense of home.

McKinley Ranch had been passed down in her family for five generations. She accepted the fact that one day the property would pass to her. A bittersweet smile tugged at her lips. True, when she was younger, she'd looked forward to the day she could raise her family here, but reality forced her to face the possibility that she would be the last McKinley to own the land.

She cursed at the unfairness of it all. In the beginning, she was a happy child. She had a beautiful mother and a successful doctor for a father. But her life took a change for the worse. One night, during a terrible storm, when she and her parents were traveling to visit McKinley Ranch her father lost control of the car.

Everything had happened so fast, yet it had seemed as if it all happened in slow motion. Christian vividly remembered her mother's scream of warning to her father, the screech of the car's tires, and the scent of burning rubber filling the air just before was she slammed hard into the front seat. Then all was quiet, too quiet.

Christian wiped away her tears. There wasn't a

day she didn't remember her parents. The pain of their deaths lessened as the years rolled by.

Her second life's tragedy occurred at the age of twenty when she discovered she had breast cancer.

Somehow, she had survived and had fallen in love with a man who had stolen more than her heart, but had promised to stand by her through thick and thin, and to treasure her always. It crushed her to know he wasn't able to keep his word. That was her life's third tragedy.

At first sight of the gazebo, she picked up the pace. The secluded spot near the pond always had a way of easing her of troubled thoughts.

A shadow caught her attention, and she stopped. Her eyes narrowed as she struggled to get a better view. A strange sensation coursed through her at the familiar span of the masculine outline and she know her visitor's identity seconds before his handsome features came into view. She froze. "Jordan?"

Nineteen

Malcolm's bored gaze scanned the ballroom, but he made sure he kept a casual smile on his face while colleagues at the conference made his acquaintance. This was the worst part of his job.

He hated networking. He glanced at his watch. Seven-thirty. *Great. The night was still young.*

When someone shook Malcolm's hand, he was prepared with a ready-made smile. The room's high volume made it impossible to hear much of anything, including the woman talking to him.

Her name tag read Barbara. She was attractive, he supposed. Pride and confidence radiated from her. However, she didn't stir his interest.

She laughed.

He laughed to accommodate her. Had she told a joke? He looked at his watch again. Seven thirty-two.

"Ah, Mal, old buddy." A deep masculine voice came from behind and cleared Malcolm's boggled haze.

He turned. A genuine smile lit his face. "Daniel!"

Daniel Finley, Malcolm's longtime friend and business associate, took his place beside him and offered his hand to the woman who still stood next to Malcolm. "Don't tell me you're hogging the most beautiful woman in the room all for yourself."

Barbara blushed.

Daniel hadn't lost his touch.

"No. Actually, Ms—"

"Collins," she offered.

"Ms. Collins and I were just enjoying a casual conversation," he said guessing. If they weren't, he'd just insulted her.

"Then that means the lady is fair game." Daniel winked, never pulling his gaze from her.

Malcolm recognized the game.

A few more compliments and a couple of smiles later, Daniel offered Barbara his arm and left Malcolm standing alone. Daniel tossed a conspiratorial wink over his shoulder at him.

Malcolm laughed and stole another glance at his watch. Seven thirty-five. The damn thing must be broken.

When he looked up, something familiar caught his attention for the briefest of moments, then vanished. He scanned the room again. A knot of apprehension settled in his gut. He didn't understand why every nerve in his body stood at attention. When his search failed to turn up anything, he dismissed his taut nerves as a symptom of jet lag.

The thought of returning to his hotel room upstairs tempted him. And for the millionth time he wondered about the purpose of these functions, then wondered how on earth Noah had talked him into taking his place.

A waiter passed and Malcolm snatched a flute of champagne. He downed the contents in a single gulp. It didn't quite pack the same punch he was used to, but beggars couldn't be choosy.

Seven forty-five.

He'd had enough. He'd smiled his last smile and had shaken his last hand for the evening. There was a bed upstairs calling his name.

He moved through the crowd with his destination cemented in his mind. Then it happened again.

He stopped.

Tense, and unsure why, he turned. The air thinned as his gaze roamed over a most beautiful set of ebony-colored shoulders and recognized them instantly.

With her back turned to him, his gaze followed the aqua-blue lining of her dress that dipped well below the center of her back.

Malcolm moved closer. His feet seemed to have a mind of their own.

She laughed.

His chest tightened at the melodious sound. It had been years, but he would've recognized the sound anywhere.

As he stood inches away, her fragrance, a soft floral scent, seduced his senses. For a few spellbinding seconds, he felt as if he'd been cast in a dream.

Alex turned and gasped as her eyes widened with recognition.

"Hello," Malcolm greeted.

Her hand flew to her mouth, and she raced past him.

Stunned, he turned and watched her disappear into the crowd. "Was it something I said?"

"Don't I at least get a hello?"

Jordan's voice poured like warm honey over Christian's chilled body. Her lips parted, but emitted no sound. When he stepped down from the gazebo, she sucked in her breath.

"I take it you're surprised to see me?" His confident smile turned seductive.

Her heart fluttered at the sight just as she discovered her voice. "What are you doing here?"

"Praying for a miracle."

The mere fact that he'd followed her to the ranch spoke volumes. Hope for their marriage widened within her, but questions still lingered.

"I've made a lot of mistakes, and I've made so many promises that I don't blame you for doubting me."

Their gazes leveled.

"I'm sorry," he added. "For so many things."

Christian caught the slight tremor in his voice.

Her eyes burned with restrained tears. "I'm sorry, too. I know how much the company means to you. I feel as if I presented you with an ultimatum—"

"Then I choose you."

Her knees weakened, and her vision blurred. Jordan moved closer. "I never meant to hurt you, or be a disappointment to you."

"You were never a disappointment."

"Then why did you leave?"

Somewhere during the course of their conversation, he'd managed to bridge the distance between them, and now his warm breath caressed her face. For a brief moment she'd forgotten the question, and had to avert her gaze to regain her bearing. "Because my ideal marriage doesn't consist of me being alone." Taking a chance, she sought his gaze again. "Because gifts don't comfort me."

Jordan closed his eyes. It wasn't the first time she'd told him this, but it was the first time he'd listened. "I guess I really screwed up."

"Yeah, I guess *we* did."

Alex splashed cold water on her face and tried to regain her composure. She stared at her reflection in the mirror. Her makeup was ruined, but she only gave it a fleeting thought before her mind centered on one terrifying image— Malcolm.

What was he doing here? He never attended these functions.

Alex caught many curious stares from the other women who drifted in and out of the women's room. She pulled her body erect and gave a few of them a quick reassuring smile. Awkwardly, she reapplied her lipstick. Once it was time to rejoin the conference reception, she hesitated.

Just ignore him. Once upon a time, Bobby had given her the advice that once you throw something away you don't go back digging through the garbage to take it out. And Alex had thrown Malcolm away years ago.

She swung open the door. Her model smile greeted everyone she passed. She made sure she drew as much attention to the blue diamond draped across her neck as possible.

The room spun beneath her feet, but she resisted the urge to reach out and steady herself. "I can get through this," she recited. Taking in a deep breath, she hoped to clear her head. Her knees weakened, then suddenly she was falling.

A pair of strong arms caught her. "I got you."

Alex's body tensed at the familiar sound of Malcolm's voice. *So much for ignoring him.*

He drew her pliant body against him, then escorted her out of the ballroom and into the gardens.

The night's cool air filled her lungs and rejuvenated much of her strength.

"Are you all right?" Malcolm led her to a nearby bench.

She nodded, unable to trust her voice.

He lowered her to the wire-frame seating, then took the vacant spot beside her.

Alex averted her gaze. Life kept landing her in one jam after another.

He turned her face toward him. "Are you sure?"

Her heart fluttered at the genuine concern laced in his eyes. Her vision blurred against her will, and despair returned.

Malcolm retrieved a handkerchief and blotted her tears. "I didn't realize you'd be this happy to see me again," he joked to lighten the mood.

She couldn't breathe, and it became harder to clear her head. "Thank you." The corners of her mouth lifted.

He returned the gesture. The silence that stretched between them was tense, yet somehow comforting.

"It's been a long time." He jump-started the conversation. Numerous questions were jumbled in his mind. It took everything he had to appear aloof when he wanted with every fiber in his body to gather her in his arms and never let go.

"Yeah, it has." She drew in a steady breath, then attempted to stand. She regretted the move the moment her stomach performed a series of somersaults.

"I think you'd better sit back down," he suggested, then eased her back onto the bench.

She couldn't believe her luck.

"I promise I won't bite," he added with a quick laugh. "Besides," he sobered, "it's past time we try to bury the hatchet. Don't you agree?"

Alex avoided his gaze again. "You make it sound so easy."

He slid his hand over hers. "It could be."

She looked up. Old yearnings returned, saturating her, while erotic thoughts filtered through her mind, and she was in no condition to fight them.

Removing his hand at her silence, Malcolm was at a loss for words.

Say something, Alex's inner voice commanded. "I really appreciate you coming to my aid in there. I guess I don't know what came over me." *Liar.*

"Don't mention it," was all he could think to say. Then he grew exasperated at his inability to draw her into a real conversation.

She took the initiative to be civil. "Do you attend many of these functions?"

Malcolm relaxed. "No. Actually Pop was supposed to attend, but had to back out at the last minute."

"Oh."

"How about you?"

"This is the third time I've attended this conference. I'm modeling Emerald Jeweler's blue diamond." She touched the base of her neck.

He laughed. "I guess that means that I'm flirting with the competition."

She arched a delicate brow.

"Come on. You must know that Emerald Jeweler's is Opulence's number one competitor."

The irony dawned on her. "So I guess that makes me the enemy," she said with a smile.

Malcolm's laughter died, but his eyes continued to hold a spark of joviality. "Never."

The dark and seductive tone of his voice caressed the core of her being. She had the sudden feeling of being in trouble. Alex returned to the subject at hand. "It's been years since I've modeled for your company."

"More like a lifetime."

Her gaze lowered to her braided fingers. "Yeah. It does feel that way."

Malcolm, armed with bravery, decided to take a chance. "You know I can't tell you how many times I've thought about this moment."

She looked up with furrowed brows.

"Well, not exactly this moment. But I've thought about what I would say if our paths crossed again."

His baritone deepened once again, and plunged her further into a strange and magical spell. Then again, she'd always felt this way around him. She blinked and took the time to return to reality. "And what had you planned to say?" she finally managed to ask.

A dimple grooved the left side of his cheek. "The exact speech eludes me now. But I know the theme was—I miss you."

Air rushed from her lungs with such a force that it brought tears to her eyes. She quickly averted her gaze. "I think I'd better go back inside." She stood, grateful that this time the ground remained steady beneath her feet.

"Please." He stood, as well. "Don't leave just yet."

Shaking her head, Alex searched for a reason to rescue her. "This is all wrong. We shouldn't be here together. It's too late for us." She turned.

Malcolm reached for her hand. "I won't be able to stand it if you walk out again."

She stopped, and remained immobile before him. She lacked the strength to leave. The evening had taken on an almost surreal quality. She would never admit that she, too, had dreamed of this moment, had also wondered what she'd say if given this opportunity. Now that the chance had arrived, she was blowing it.

Malcolm moved closer.

She felt his firm chest pressed against her back. Every limb on her body trembled. Everything was moving too fast.

"Please stay."

His simple request hung on the night's air and tore at her heart.

Alex brushed her hand against her stomach. She lost the battle to control her tears, and turned to face him as they slid from her eyes. "I can't. We can't go back. Things are different now, I'm a different person."

Malcolm reached and brushed the dewy tracks from her face. "I'm not suggesting that we dive into anything. But you can't tell me that you don't still care for me. I can feel that you do."

"It doesn't matter. A lot has changed."

He withdrew his hand. "Is there someone else?"

She would have laughed at the absurdity of his question had it not depressed her. "No. It's nothing like that. It's—"

He stared, dumbfounded at her sudden rush of tears, but he recovered and enfolded her into his arms. That was where he longed for her to be. That was where she belonged, whether she knew it or not.

Her body's trembling turned violent, and he wondered at the true source of her strange behavior. He waited a long time for her tears to subside, and knew that he'd wait for as long as it took.

Embarrassment burned her cheeks as she pulled from his arms "I'm sorry. I guess I'm not feeling quite like myself tonight."

"What's wrong?" His gaze bored into hers.

She shrugged and tried to come up with a lie, but she couldn't.

"You know once upon a time we were the best of friends. I'd love nothing more than to be that friend to you now." He closed what little distance she'd established between them. "Please tell me what's really troubling you tonight."

Her heart trusted him, her soul needed him, and her confession fell from her lips before she gave it another thought. "I'm pregnant."

Twenty

Christian and Jordan sat huddled inside the quaint gazebo well into the night. They gazed up at the stars and commented on how everything seemed brighter—clearer.

They knew there were no quick fixes for their problems, but neither wanted a divorce.

"When I saw you tonight, I thought I'd somehow stepped back in time," she said, lying against him as she continued to stargaze.

He smiled. "I knew you'd show up down here sooner or later. I just didn't know whether Pete would give me away or not."

"I should have known." She laughed, remembering Pete's speech.

"I don't know," he continued. "I guess I'd hoped to rekindle the magic." His fingers threaded through her hair. "This place does hold a lot of memories."

She lifted her head. "I always feel magic whenever we're together. I still get those funny butterflies whenever you look at me, as you're doing now."

"And I'm still very much in love with you," he replied tenderly. He caressed her cheek.

She kissed his hand and thought for a moment. "The question is whether it's enough."

His hands lowered as a wounded look struck his features.

She inched closer. "I know you love me. I really do. And I love you. But yet I'm unhappy. There's something wrong with this equation."

"I never meant for that to happen."

"I know." Her voice cracked. However, the reality of her life didn't resemble the one she'd dreamed of as a child. True, she had her knight in shining armor, but what happened to the happily ever after part? "Maybe we've done all that we can, or have tried all there is to try."

"No," he said with a firm headshake. "I don't believe that."

An ache swelled her heart as fresh tears crested her lashes. "Let's face it. What am I asking you to do—give up your company?" She pressed a silencing finger against his lips before he could interrupt. "I can't ask you to do that. It's too much a part of who you are. I truly understand that."

At the finality in her voice, the straightening of her back, and the lift of her chin, desperation seized Jordan.

"What do you want? What will it take to make you happy?"

Her vision blurred at the sight of his eyes glistening in the moonlight. Love radiated from them and for the first time, broke her heart.

He pulled her into his arms.

Christian's tears fell as she leaned forward.

He lowered his head until their foreheads pressed together.

"Sweetheart, it's not about you doing what *I* want you to do." She broke contact to toss up her hands. "I know this sounds like a bag of contradictions. And I wish I had the answers. I just know I can't continue to live this way. Something has to change."

He nodded, then said in a firm voice, "I know we deserve to be together. The company doesn't mean a damn thing if you're not there to share it with me. You have to believe that."

Christian hesitated.

Jordan jumped to his feet and slammed his hands into his pockets. "I admit I've been driven most of my life to succeed. That's no secret. But I know it's gone into extremes in the last few years. I needed to prove something to myself. I needed to prove something to Noah, and even to you, too." He shrugged. "Why is it so wrong to want to give you the best, and want you to do anything and everything your heart desires?"

His confession added new questions. "Is that the reason you financed *Nuwoman Publications*?"

"It was something you wanted. It seemed that it was the only thing I was capable of giving you. I want to fill our lives with something since we can't have . . ."

The force of his unspoken words seized the air from her lungs. Her heart shattered, and was reflected in her pained expression. She stood, then thought better of the notion and sat back down.

He rushed to her side. "I didn't mean that the way it—"

"Yes you did." She nodded. "That's what's really between us, isn't it? The fact that we may never have children," she said, convinced reality was staring her in the face.

"Chris—"

"Can you deny it?"

His slight hesitation became her answer. She slammed her eyes shut. "Oh God, Jordan."

Once again he moved to comfort her, only to have her ward off his efforts.

Shame, anger, and a deep sense of incompetence coursed through her. She turned, giving him her back.

"Baby, please. I didn't mean to say that. I just—"

"No." She shook her head. "I'm glad it's finally out in the open." Her hands trembled as she wiped her tears. "I'm just surprised it's taken us this long."

His gaze lowered at the anguish in her expression. "I can't seem to get this right."

"Maybe we're just asking for the impossible," she admitted when her courage restored.

He looked up. "Don't say that."

"Let's face it, I may never be able to have children."

"I don't care," he reinforced.

"Yes, you do." She reached for his hand. "You deserve children."

"Then let's adopt."

She fell silent. In the past he wouldn't accept the idea of adoption. He was always so confident that the next fertility drug would work. Now, the sudden announcement floored her.

"Yes, why don't we?" he continued as he brushed a strand of hair from her eyes.

"I feel as if I've failed you," she whispered.

"Never."

Their gazes locked, and for a brief moment she couldn't think of a reason why they shouldn't, but then she remembered. "I don't want to raise a child alone. You're never home—"

"I'll cut back on my workload," he swore. His enthusiasm heightened as he warmed to the idea.

For the first time, her doubts faded, and hope flourished.

"But it can't be this simple."

"It can be if we let it."

She hesitated.

"Say yes," he encouraged.

His sincerity won her over, and her answer came quickly. "Yes."

Malcolm gathered Alexandria into his arms and reveled in the fact that she'd allowed him to comfort her. For the next few hours he listened to her telling of her short-lived love affair with some Robert character. For Malcolm, it seemed as if they'd slipped back in time, and were once again the best of friends who told each other everything.

Yet, as he listened, an overpowering sense of jealousy wrenched his heart, and he couldn't help but wish that it were his child growing inside of her. The night played like a scene from a dream. They strolled around the hotel's grounds, oblivious to the flurry of activity around them.

Alex glanced at him and felt the need to kick herself. She couldn't believe that she'd just unburdened herself of her troubles to him. It had always been this way between them. It was only when they'd tried to turn their friendship into something more that it had blown up in their faces.

As they talked as they did now, something more than friendship resurfaced. Perhaps it was the way he looked at her. She felt beautiful, desirable, and more importantly, wanted.

"I think you'll make a wonderful mother," Malcolm assured her.

They'd stopped near the gardens.

"I sure hope so." She hugged herself in an attempt to ward off the night's slight chill.

"Here." He removed his jacket and slid it around her shoulders.

The scent of his cologne weakened her knees. "Thank you."

Their gazes locked.

Malcolm stared at the woman who ruled every corner of his heart as desire threatened his control. He didn't want to do anything that could destroy the moment. "I've missed you."

Speechless, she averted her gaze.

"Why have you ignored me all these years?"

Alex started to deny the accusation, but knew there was no point. "You know why."

"No, I don't." His voice lowered. "You knew how I felt. I think what hurt the most is that you thought the worst, then didn't give me the chance to explain what truly happened."

She turned, but he placed a restraining hand against her arm.

"I've had plenty of time to think about this. Do you want to know what I concluded?"

She shook her head.

"I'll tell you anyway." He moved closer, his fingers lifting her chin, enabling their gazes to meet. "I think you were looking for a reason to leave. Maybe my reputation scared you."

She didn't respond. She couldn't.

"I'm right, aren't I?"

It was a fact she'd refused to even acknowledge to herself. Malcolm's reputation with women had been well-earned, and no one knew it better than she did. The fact that he'd proposed to Christian just one week before he'd confessed to being in love with her only added to her doubts.

"Alex, talk to me."

"I don't know what you want me to say." She turned her face away and looked down.

"Only the truth."

She felt exposed and perhaps vulnerable. "It would have never worked." To her surprise, he laughed. She looked up. "What's so funny?"

"We are," he replied, shaking his head.

She smiled, but felt a need to confess. "I've missed you, too."

He sobered.

"I guess we'll never know what we threw away." A hint of hope lingered in her voice, and she wondered if he'd heard it.

"I wouldn't say that."

His smoldering gaze caressed her face. And despite the earlier chill, her body warmed.

"Seems to me there's still a bond between us that even time can't destroy." He inched closer. "What do you think?"

She couldn't think with him looking at her like that. "It felt good talking to you tonight. It's brought back a lot of memories. I miss having you as a friend."

He moved closer. His warm breath brushed against her face. "Maybe there's still something between us."

Helplessly affected by the husky timbre of his voice, the sensuality of his eyes, she leaned forward as if his body were a large magnet. Alex's last vestige of resistance crumbled as her gaze lowered to his lips.

The moment their lips touched, the sweetest

sensation coursed through her. She closed her eyes and savored his taste. Had it not been for his steel embrace, she would have fallen at his feet. One thing remained certain—there was still a strong bond between them. Her dilemma now was whether she wanted to risk love again.

Their kiss deepened, and her answer flowed from her heart: *Oh, yes.*

Twenty-one

As a minivacation, Jordan and Christian decided to stay at McKinley Ranch for the next week. The entire family managed to elicit a promise from Jordan not to call his office. And to his utter amazement, no one tried to reach him.

By the third day, he was tempted to call. He also resented the sleeping arrangements—Christian insisted on separate rooms while they worked through their problems. At first it sounded like a reasonable request, but he'd hoped the separation wouldn't last the full week.

On the fourth day, his body ached in places he'd long forgotten existed. He didn't know why Pete had asked him for his help breaking in some new thoroughbreds. Worse than that, he didn't know why on earth he'd agreed.

The alarm clock sounded—5:00 A.M.

He closed his eyes and prayed it wasn't true. Before he could turn it off, a loud knock sounded at the door.

"Rise and shine, city boy," Pete's voice boomed. "See you down at breakfast."

Jordan groaned. The older man's energy amazed him. Forcing himself up to lean against the pillows, he once again thought of calling the office, but another knock distracted him.

Christian poked her head around the door. "Good morning."

"That all depends on whether I can keep my butt off a horse."

She laughed and entered. "Why don't you just tell Pete no?"

"Are you kidding? That man's trying to break me, and I refuse to give him the satisfaction."

"I think Pete has a speech on pride that you'd be very interested to hear."

"I've heard it."

She smiled. "All right. But you know what Bobby always says—'A hard head makes a soft butt.' "

"Or a sore one," he corrected.

She laughed until he stood up from the bed nude. It had been a long time, she reminded herself as he headed toward the adjoining bathroom. She waited until the door closed before fanning herself with her hand. Some of her husband's best attributes were coming back to her now.

Later at breakfast, Pete regaled them with humorous stories of Jordan's falls and blunders. And despite his obvious embarrassment, Jordan took the harassment with genuine smile.

As Christian watched the light exchange, she wished she could somehow bottle his joviality and take it back to Atlanta with them. How he'd managed to transform into the man who had stolen her heart so long ago remained a mystery. But who was she to look a gift horse in the mouth?

"So, Chrissy tells me that you guys are looking into adoption." Bobby cut through the men's idle chatter to lock gazes with Jordan.

He quickly looked to Christian.

"Sorry," she whispered for his ears only. They'd agreed to tell the family together once they worked out everything, but it was too big a secret for Christian to keep.

"Yes, ma'am." Jordan smiled.

"Well, it's about time, if you ask me." Pete tilted his hat up and nodded toward the couple with a spreading grin.

"How many times do I have to tell you about this?" Bobby snatched his hat off his head and sent the small group into fits of laughter.

"Now, I done told you I feel naked without my hat."

"And I done told you the rules at this table. You make up your own mind whether you want to be naked, or want to starve."

Knowing exactly which battles he could and couldn't win, Pete returned his attention to Jordan and Christian. "Well, I think that's great news. Why haven't you two said anything? Hell, that's sounds like a reason to celebrate."

"That's mighty kind of you," Jordan mimicked Pete's accent perfectly, causing another ripple of laughter at the table. "But it's not necessary." He squeezed his wife's hand.

"Ah, come on," Bobby interrupted. "It's the first time in years we've seen you two down here together. We're looking for any reason to throw a nice little get-together."

With that said, the couple knew nothing would change her mind. Throughout the rest of their meal, the other family members planned the celebration. However, Christian didn't understand how forty people could be considered a small group.

That evening, Pete and Dylan returned to the house with four other wranglers, carrying Jordan on their shoulders as if they were carrying a gurney.

Christian's eyes widened in horror as she raced down the staircase. "What happened?"

Jordan groaned.

"Aw, he'll be all right," Pete reassured. "He just had a little trouble with one of the horses, is all. I'm sure after a nice hot bath and a good night's sleep he'll be as right as rain."

She followed them back up the stairs to the guest room. When they placed Jordan on the bed, she saw for the first time that he was covered with dirt.

She grabbed her uncle's arm before he could escape. "Why do you always ask him to do these crazy things? You know he's not experienced."

"Aw, now Chrissy. He's all right. Me and the guys were just having a little fun with him."

"Trying to kill him is having a little fun?"

His smile fell. "Now you know I would never do anything to deliberately hurt him. You know he's my favorite city boy."

His light humor fell on deaf ears. Though she knew he didn't mean any harm, it didn't make it any easier to see her husband in such pain. She turned away from her uncle in order to regain control of her temper.

He touched her shoulder gently. "I'm sorry."

"It's all right." She exhaled. "I shouldn't have snapped at you. I know you mean well."

She waited until the door closed before she returned to Jordan's side.

He rolled his head in her direction and smiled. "I think you've just ruined my reputation."

Slapping her hands against her hips, she stared at him with disbelief. "Which reputation is that—the one of a rodeo clown?"

He shook his head as if she didn't understand.

"You have to be kidding me, Jordan. You could have been killed out there trying to play cowboy."

His brows wiggled as amusement lit his eyes. "I love it when you worry about me."

Then, to her utter amazement, he sat up in bed without a flinch. "What on earth?" Her eyes narrowed. "Why, you big fake!"

His hands covered his heart. "Who, me?"

She grabbed a pillow and whacked him soundly

in the face. "How dare you scare me like me that? And how could you just let me cuss my uncle out like that?"

He laughed. "If you ask me, he deserved it. You even said yourself he was trying to kill me."

His burst of laughter infuriated her. She jumped on the bed and continued to pound him with the pillow until, in defense, he returned fire.

Christian laughed for a brief moment when she believed she was winning, then shrieked in mock horror when the tables were turned.

"Had enough?" he asked, sending another whack to her body.

Her efforts at a counterattack proved worthless, and she cried out in desperation. "Yes!"

Jordan cast his pillow aside with a look of triumph and arrogance. "It's about time."

In a last attempt to save face, she took a final swing with her pillow.

The unexpected attack caught him off guard and swept him over the side of the bed. His body hit the floor with a loud thump.

Shocked and amused, she rolled over, glanced down at the floor and saw him rubbing the side of his head. She snickered, then tried to muffle the outburst. "Are you all right?"

His eyes narrowed. "I'm going to get you for that." He leaped toward the bed.

She screamed and jerked away, barely escaping her husband's grasp when she sprang from the bed.

A game of cat and mouse ensued as he chased her around the room. Neither heard the knock at the door, but when Bobby entered Christian seized the opportunity to use her grandmother's body as a shield.

"What in tarnation are you two doing in here?" She screamed, as well, when Jordan lunged toward her in a desperate move to reach Christian.

He missed.

"I'm going to get you," he threatened in a low whisper.

"Will you two behave?" Bobby fanned herself as Christian continued to turn her body this way and that, still dodging Jordan.

"No," Christian screamed when his hand landed on her wrist and dragged her from behind her grandmother. Then, in one quick swoop, he tossed her over his shoulder.

"I think I can handle things from here," he informed Bobby with a wink, as if she'd asked.

She shook her head. "You younguns," she mumbled, and closed the bedroom door behind her.

"Put me down." Christian pounded his back, fearful of what he might do. She didn't have long to find out.

He returned to the bed with her and draped her over his knee.

When she realized his intent, she struggled to break free, but to no avail. The first smack to her backside sent a wave of shock through her. "Let me up!"

"Not until you apologize."

"Never!" The next whack stung. "Jordan, this isn't funny."

"Speak for yourself."

Whack.

"Stop," she begged as her outrage gave way to humiliation.

"Are you going to apologize?"

"No."

Whack.

"Jordan, please."

"Say you're sorry."

"Go to hell."

Whack.

"All right. I'm sorry." She jolted out of his lap the instant he released her. Her butt burned so much she feared sitting down.

He leaned back across the bed, grinning like a Cheshire cat. "We ought to that more often. I rather enjoyed it."

"I just bet you did." She pouted as she rubbed the tender area. "That hurt."

He frowned with false sympathy as he caught her by the wrist and dragged her onto the bed. "Aw. Let me kiss it and make it all better."

Malcolm's eyes widened as the waiter placed what seemed like half the items on the menu on the table. "Are you going to eat all of that?"

"Doesn't it look divine?" Alex closed her eyes and inhaled her dinner's heavenly aroma. "I'm starving."

"I'd say that was obvious." He crossed his arms. "Now *this* I have to see."

She looked over at him. "Don't tell me you're just going to sit there and watch me eat."

"We all have our forms of entertainment."

"Ha, ha." She gave him a quick smile, then took her first bite of the salmon.

Her moan of sheer pleasure caught him off guard, and the sight of her eyes drifting closed was one of the most erotic things he'd ever seen. *Just friends,* he recited to himself, even though they'd been inseparable in the last week.

It was a start, he reasoned, and he was grateful. If everything went as planned, they'd be engaged by the holidays.

A mother.

He smiled at the delightful thought, and held no doubts that she'd be a wonderful mother . . . and wife.

She took another bite of her food, and he thought he'd go insane listening to her continuous moans. Memories of her being locked in his embrace along with the sweet taste of her lips had his emotions twisted in knots, making it nearly impossible to sit still.

He desperately needed a drink or a cigarette—he didn't care which.

"You really ought to try this." She cut a piece and offered him a plump portion on her fork.

Malcolm lowered his head, yet kept his gaze locked with hers.

To Alex, his slow and deliberate motion to open his mouth and accept the morsel almost seemed wicked. And, as if in retaliation, he made a low seductive moan that did, in fact, curl her toes.

"You're right. It is good."

Alex's mouth went dry, and her mind drew a blank. Had he said something? She blinked and broke her dream-like trance. "Just friends," she reaffirmed.

"What did you say?"

Damn. Had she said that aloud? "Nothing," she lied, then tried to regain her composure.

He smiled. "So, how did your doctor's appointment go?"

The change of subject brought an instant smile. "Great. I had my obstetric profile done. You know, this is really exciting."

"When will we know what the baby's sex is?"

"In my fifth month. But I don't care what it is—I'm just praying for ten fingers and toes."

Malcolm enjoyed her excitement, and continued to suppress his jealousy. "Well, I'm happy for you."

She covered his hands with hers. "Thanks so much for being here for me. I can't tell you how much I appreciate it."

"This is where I'm supposed to be." This time

when their gazes locked a strange sensation flowed through them. "Remember," he added. "Never hesitate to ask for anything. I'll always be here for you."

Twenty-two

Christian gripped the headboard as Jordan cupped her buttocks and drew her close. When his hot mouth invaded the dewy haven between her thighs, she quivered and twisted beneath him, drifting hazily between two worlds.

Spasms of euphoria stole her breath, causing her to arch. The maneuver gained him better access to her body's core. Her grip tightened as she moaned in pleasure, submerging further into a sea of sweet oblivion.

Jordan surfaced and shared the taste of her orgasm through a deep, sensual kiss. When the kiss ended, he held her while she continued to tremble in the aftermath of her climax.

However, he didn't let her rest for long. His next touch surged like familiar fire through her, and scorched a trail of desire down the valley of her breasts. His potent lips created a passion-filled haze and kept her dizzy with desire.

It had always been this way between them. Their bodies knew what they needed, and every curve seemed predestined to fit.

Jordan raided the hollow point of her throat, causing her world to spiral out of control as pulses of heat vibrated the core of her being.

He reveled in the scent of jasmine absorbed in her skin, and he melted into her fiery kisses. At first, she was soft and yielding, then turned hot and aggressive.

Her tongue flicked against his nipples, and he held his breath to stifle his gasps. His control threatened to desert him when her mouth persisted to explore other areas of his body. Her teasing soon became an agony of unendurable torment.

When her mouth closed around his hard shaft and then proceeded to devour every inch, his thoughts were muddled, and sanity finally abandoned him. The erotic rhythm she created made it almost impossible for him to catch his breath.

Not ready to end the moment with an early explosion, he forced her up, then settled his hands against her hips as she mounted. Her slick entry welcomed him, and he had to grit his teeth to prevent another potential explosion.

"Please, don't stop," he begged, lifting higher and deeper into her tight, wet warmth. In a flash, he seized the dominant position and challenged her to match his wild pace.

Christian's moans intensified and increased in volume, while her hands slid down the muscular cords of his back, then dug her nails into its soft flesh.

A low growl tumbled from his lips in a combination of pain and pleasure. He grabbed her hands and held them over her head, locked in his fist. He found and sucked on a taut nipple.

Christian couldn't think, and wasn't sure she wanted to. Mindless to her incoherent chatter, she only knew that if he stopped, she'd die.

Gradually, his breath came in shallow gusts of air.

Again, she arched into his thrust, striving toward a pinnacle just beyond her reach. Suddenly, a blistering heat swept through her, and in the same instant Jordan's hold tightened as he groaned his release.

They lay still for a moment, still intimately joined while suspended in a gauzy web of warm serenity.

"We should never leave this bed," Jordan said when his breathing returned to normal. He rolled to his side and pulled her against him.

"Wouldn't that be wonderful?" She snuggled closer.

He brushed back a damp lock of hair from her face, then kissed her.

A lazy smile curved on her lips as her eyes fluttered open.

His dark eyes impaled her. "I don't think I'll ever be able to show or express just how much I love you," he said in a hoarse voice thickened by desire.

"I don't know about that. If tonight was any indication, I'd say you expressed it perfectly."

He laughed. "If we're judging by tonight's performances. I'd say you're crazy about me, too."

"Insanely."

He sat up in bed and reached over to the nightstand. When he returned his attention to her, she eyed him suspiciously.

"What is it?"

He hesitated for a moment before replying. "There's something I'm dying to give you. But before I can, I need to know if we're going to try a hundred percent to rebuild our marriage. I know we've discussed a lot of things, and I think we've both concluded there's no way we can really live without each other."

Christian sat up, recognizing his words to be true.

"I'm promising you right now that I'll never place anything or anyone above you again."

"And I promise to support you more, and to be a little more patient and understanding," she responded, gazing into his eyes.

"Then I believe these belong to you." Jordan opened his hand and revealed her wedding rings.

Her eyes filled with tears as he slid them back onto her finger.

He gathered her into his arms, then branded her with a kiss.

Seconds later, they went into round two of their sexual frenzy.

* * *

Alex faced her bedroom window and stared out into the night. New feelings mixed with old filled her with a sense of hope, not only for herself, but also for her child.

She didn't presume Malcolm was her answer to anything. In fact, she realized it wasn't realistic for her to jump from one relationship into another. However, she'd gained closure on an old chapter in her life and, as a result, she had her old friend back.

Their friendship was different than the one she held with Chris. She didn't know how, exactly. She could tell them both anything, but Malcolm had always seemed an extension of herself.

That thought lingered in her mind, its meaning almost too powerful to ignore. She shook her head. She was behaving like a hopeless romantic, and that wasn't like her. Looking toward the future, she promised herself to keep an open mind and an open heart.

Christian gazed at her husband lying beside her and studied his handsome features. She felt closer to him than she had in years.

A baby. They were actually going to pursue adoption. She couldn't believe it. The thought thrilled her. And as surely as she needed air to breathe, she knew this was the missing piece in their lives' jigsaw puzzle.

Jordan's promises echoed in her mind, and for the first time in a long while she believed he'd fulfill them.

Twenty-three

Two months later

Christian waited inside the front door at Planet Hollywood in the middle of downtown Atlanta, ecstatic about the opportunity to see Alex after such a long absence. Modeling still had her friend traveling quite a bit, though she swore she'd quit soon.

Between Jordan, adoption centers, and *Nuwoman* magazine, Christian had managed to maintain contact over the phone.

Alex glided through the door dressed in a stunning winter-white pantsuit, looking the part of a famous runway model.

"You look great," Christian greeted with a bright smile and a tight hug.

"Me? Look at you, Mrs. Givenchy."

"Good eye."

"I know my designers," Alex boasted. "But I'm being for real, girl. You're practically glowing. What's up?"

"What can I say—life's wonderful." Her brows wiggled as a mischievous gleam lit her eyes.

"I just bet it is, but you'd better knock on wood. Murphy's Law has a way of jerking the fun out of life."

The hostess interrupted the women's excited chatter and escorted them to their table. Once seated, they slid back into easy conversation.

"I can't believe you're almost five months pregnant. Look at your little pouch. It looks as if you swallowed a small cantaloupe."

"Ha, ha. Everyone wants to be a comedian." Alex rolled her eyes heavenward. "I swear, I've worried the hell out of my doctor in the last month alone concerning one thing or another. But she's assured me that I'm going to have a normal and healthy baby."

Christian bubbled with happiness. "I can hardly wait. I'm the godmother, right?"

"Of course. Oh, I almost forgot." She reached for her purse. "I brought the latest ultrasound pictures. Do you want to see them?"

"I'd love to." Christian moved her chair over to the table's edge to get a better view.

The women poured over the black-and-white still photos, trying their best to distinguish one body part from another.

"I can't believe it. You're going to have a little boy. Any clue to what you'll name him?"

"None. But I've bought ten baby name books."

"Well, just make sure I can pronounce it, or at least spell it."

Alex laughed. "I promise. But I can hardly wait. At the first chance you get, you must come and see the stuff we bought for the nursery. Malcolm said he picked out a crib. I can't wait to see it."

Christian's brows lifted. She couldn't remember the last time she'd seen her friend this happy or excited about anything, and something told her it was more than the pregnancy. "It's funny you should mention Malcolm. I just saw him myself the other day. He's seems . . . happier than normal lately."

"Oh?" Alex shrugged.

Christian burst into laughter.

"What's so funny?"

"You are. I can't believe you weren't going to tell me!"

Alex opened her mouth.

"And don't bother to deny it. Malcolm has already told me."

"He *didn't*." Her eyes rounded.

"Okay, maybe I tricked him into confessing." Christian shrugged. "Either way, you don't need to bother with this silly charade."

"All right. So you caught me." Alex's eyes danced as a sly smile appeared. "So what did he say?"

"Hold on. One thing at a time. Why did you hide this from me? I think it's great you two finally got back together."

The waiter's timing couldn't have been more perfect. Their conversation was temporarily placed on hold as he asked for their orders. While Alex inquired about different items, she kept her eyes averted, which only agitated Christian.

Being a picky eater, Alex had ordered just about everything on the side, and substituted one thing for another. All the while, Christian thought events from the Book of Revelations would begin before her friend finished.

After their orders were placed, she playfully slapped Alex's hand. "Now, tell me. What's with all the secrecy?"

A deep shade of burgundy colored Alex's face. "You know I try not to kiss and tell."

"You told me you were pregnant. And, correct me if I'm wrong, but the last time I checked that involves a hell of a lot more than kissing. Come on, this is me you're talking to."

"I know." She exhaled, then averted her gaze again. "There's really nothing to tell. We've gone out a few times, but I think we're just focusing on rebuilding our friendship at this point."

"Uh, huh." Christian crossed her arms. "And you're not the slightest bit interested in pursuing this any further?"

Alex hesitated.

"Ah, ha!" She clapped her hands, then pointed at her embarrassed friend. "You need to try to fool someone else, because I know you. And I've known for the last fifteen years, despite your flippant attitude, you're still in love with this man. And from what I've seen he's in love with you, too."

Silent, Alex mulled over her friend's words. "I just don't want to get my hopes up, you know? And besides, I have other things I need to concentrate on right now. If it works out, then great. If not, I have to be prepared for that, as well."

"I understand. I'll let it go for now, but sooner or later I'll get the details."

Alex turned the tables. "So, what did you and Malcolm talk about?"

"Ah, so now you want to try to get information from me?"

Hiding her annoyance, Alex switched tactics. "All right, don't tell me." She shrugged. "Tell me, what's been going on with you and Jordan?"

Christian's brows furrowed with suspicion. "You're really not interested in what Malcolm had to say?"

"Not if you feel like it's betraying his trust or something. Besides," she added confidently, "there's really nothing to say."

"I don't believe you," Christian concluded.

"Whatever." Alex relaxed. "Now, what about you?"

Christian played along. "Well, as you know, Jordan and I have been visiting different adoption centers. But I've got to tell you, this process is harder than I thought. Not to mention that I've fallen in love with every child I've seen. I wish you could read some of these children's profiles."

"I can imagine."

"Then there's all this paperwork that asks a million and one questions." She smiled contentedly to herself. "But I'm having the time of my life. I just know in the end it'll all be worth it."

"Won't it be great?" Alex chimed in with a dreamy expression. "Both of us being mothers at the same time."

"It'll be wonderful."

After the food arrived, they quickly resumed their conversation.

"How's Jordan's schedule been working out?"

"I have to be honest. It's a struggle for him to relinquish control at times, but I'm happy to report that he's kept his promise. He's delegated a lot of his workload. Last night he was talking about promoting Quentin Elliott."

Alex frowned as she struggled to recall. "Why does that name sound familiar?"

"Oh, I'm sure you've heard me mention him from time to time over the years. He's been with the company since the very beginning. Jordan trusts him with his life. I don't know. I think he's a nice guy. I'm hoping he does promote him."

"Sounds like a woman with a secret agenda."

"Precisely. Anything that'll free up Jordan's time, I'm all for it."

"Sounds like everything has worked out for both of us."

Christian nodded. "It sure looks that way."

"Then, let's make a toast." Alex said lifting her glass of club soda.

"What shall we toast to? To happy endings."

"Here, here."

Unable to suppress her curiosity any longer, Alex finally asked, "Now—what did Malcolm tell you?"

Christian laughed.

During the drive back to the office, Christian made several business calls, trying to orchestrate numerous tasks and rearrange meetings. She made every effort to make sure she practiced what she preached. She and Jordan had agreed to have dinner together at least three times a week—unless of course, one or the other was out of town.

Everything she'd said to Alex tonight was true. Jordan had kept his word, and he was equally excited, if not more, about the possibility of adoption.

She glanced at her watch. She had plenty of time to make her two o'clock meeting. Returning her attention to the road, she felt her vision blur. "What the hell?" Startled, she swerved, then regained control of the car.

The next moment, her eyesight cleared and she pulled to the side of the road. Her heart pounded. It was the third time this week it had happened. She rested her head on the steering wheel and noticed a bright red spot in the crotch of her pants.

"Great." Her irregular periods lately were becoming a major irritation. Glancing at her watch, she had to chance running to the house for a quick change.

She eased back onto the main road. If she had to delay her meeting, she would be the one late for dinner tonight. "Now that would be a change of pace." She laughed, then rushed to make it home.

It was days before Christian scheduled a doctor's appointment. In the meantime, she'd hoped her abnormal spotting would go away, but instead she developed other strange symptoms. However, she did relax after reading an article on how stress often affected a woman's menstrual cycle.

But nothing could have prepared her for the doctor's diagnosis.

"I'm what?"

"Pregnant." Dr. McNally peered over the rim of his glasses. "Are you all right?"

She sat on the edge of her chair and stared at him. She half-expected him to end the sentence with, "I'm just joking."

He never did.

When the news slowly sank in, a strange combination of disbelief and excitement stirred in her. "When? How?"

He laughed. "I'm not exactly privy to the when part, and I sincerely hope you *do* know about the how. But what I can tell you is that your gestation is approximately eight weeks."

"Two months? How's that possible? I'm still getting my monthly periods."

"That's not so unusual. Women's bodies often react differently. But you are most definitely pregnant."

Christian slapped her hands across her mouth as tears trickled from her eyes. "Please, say this isn't a dream."

"It's not a dream. Congratulations, Mrs. Williams."

She stood and flung her arms around him. "Oh, thank you."

Another rumble of laughter shook his body. "I'm hardly the one to thank."

When she pulled back, she read something else in his expression. "What is it?"

He smiled again, but this time she noticed it seemed forced. "I don't want to alarm you, but we detected something else."

Twenty-four

Jordan paced the floor of his office. Occasionally, he glanced at the flat screen television at the news coverage of Compucom System's phenomenal new software package. Experts were already calling the system an innovative breakthrough for the next millennium.

He couldn't believe Michael Andrews had actually beaten him to the punch. It was a hard blow for J.W. Enterprises, and it showed in their sudden drop in the stock market.

Through it all, Jordan handled the defeat well—or so he'd tried to convince himself. His employees, on the other hand, held a different view.

Charlotte buzzed over the line.

"What is it?" He couldn't hear the razor-sharp edge in his voice, but he picked up his secretary's irritation.

"I have Mr. Andrews on line one."

He thought of using the 'in a meeting' excuse, but decided to go ahead and take his medicine. "Thanks. Send the call through."

He clicked off the television and picked up the phone. "Jordan Williams."

Leaning back in his chair, he drew a deep breath.

"Ah, Jordy," Michael exclaimed. "You didn't happen to catch the news today?"

"If you called to gloat, Mikey, make it quick." He glanced at his watch. "I have more important things to attend to this afternoon."

Sweat drenched Malcolm's body as he applied the second coat of paint to the nursery. Anticipation of Alex's surprised expression brought a smile to his face. Remembering her casual comment of wanting the baby's room done in Passion Blue, he'd decided to do it.

Of course, he could have hired someone, but he took pride in the project, despite the small errors blotted along the ceiling. For his first job, he thought he'd done rather well.

The doorbell rang.

He glanced at his watch. Jordan had promised to help him pick up the baby crib he'd selected. Placing the roller into the pan, he wiped his hands on his paint splattered jeans, then he went to answer the door.

Treading across the apartment, he was careful not to touch anything. "You're early, Bro," he said as he swung the door open, but realized his mistake at the sight of a tailored-dressed gentleman holding a bunch of roses.

"I'm sorry. I thought you were someone else." Malcolm's gaze raked his visitor. "Can I help you?"

"Just who in the hell are you?"

Taken aback by the man's hostility, Malcolm felt his stance turn combative. "That's none of your business."

As he eased his shades down to set at the tip of his nose, the man's onyx eyes pierced Malcolm with a murderous glare. "Don't tell me Alex has already found a new toy." He pushed the sunglasses back in place. "And a hired hand, at that."

Malcolm saw red, and quickly concluded the visitor's identity. His hackles stood on end as his hands balled at his sides. "You have until the count of three to tell me what you want or to get the hell out."

"Touché." Robert took a bold step through the entrance and handed the roses to Malcolm. "I'm here to talk to Alex." He shrugged, then mumbled under his breath. "That's if she still insists on going through with this harebrained idea."

A lethal rage shook Malcolm to the core. "Like I said, my fiancée isn't here."

The man's chiseled features crumbled. "Your fiancée?" He eyed him suspiciously. "I think I would know whether or not Alex is engaged."

"A lot can happen in two months," Malcolm bluffed.

"I take it she's told you about me."

"Yeah, I see there are a few details she left out," he said with open contempt as he held the door open. "I'll make sure I tell her you came by."

Robert refused to be intimidated. "I didn't quite catch your name."

"Malcolm Williams."

"Ah, I *do* know you." He removed his shades and narrowed his gaze. "Alex told me all about discovering you with another woman." He laughed. "So you finally managed to weasel your way back into her life?"

Malcolm slammed the door and tossed the roses across the room.

"Don't get me wrong." Robert held up his hands in surrender, while retreating. "It's not like I don't understand. I'm sure we both can agree she's quite a woman." He continued to back away as Malcolm stormed toward him.

"Let's get one thing straight. My relationship with Alex is none of your damn business."

"It's cool, it's cool." Robert stopped. "But if you don't mind, I think I'll still wait until she returns."

"I mind."

"She's carrying *my* child. I have every right to be here. We have a few things we need to discuss. *In private.*"

The muscles along Malcolm's jaw twitched. "Don't tell me you finally grew a backbone, and are going to provide for your child?"

He didn't respond.

"I see." Malcolm shook his head and guessed. "Or maybe you expected to convince her to abort?" At the man's hesitation, he laughed before adding, "You're more pathetic than I thought."

Robert took a threatening step forward.

Malcolm matched his move.

"You know, now that I think about it, I don't know why I should even believe the kid is mine," Robert sneered. "How do I know she's telling the truth? The kid could be yours, for all I know."

"Are you suddenly the poster child for honesty? Tell me, how's the wife doing?"

Robert's eyes blazed. "My wife is none of your damn business."

"Touché." Malcolm itched for a fight. "I wouldn't be too sure about that. From what I know of Sandy, I'd say she'd find all your, shall we say, extramarital activities very interesting."

"How in the hell do you know my wife?"

"Let's just say I made it a point to know her."

"How in the hell?" Robert took another step. "You've been following me around," he accused.

Malcolm's grin widened. He had hired a private investigator as added insurance that this jerk wasn't a threat. "Anything concerning Alex concerns me. Including the child she's carrying."

"You shouldn't put your nose where it doesn't belong," Robert raged.

"Are you threatening me?

"You're damned right I am."

"Well, let me make you a few promises." Malcolm moved so close that they were just inches apart. "If I even think you've been in contact with Alex again, not only will your wife learn of our child—"

"*Our* child? What the hell is this? Are you saying you're the father?"

"No. I'm not the biological father. But I have every intention of marrying Alex, and that means adopting the baby."

"You have to be joking."

"That's right. I'm the one the kid will be calling Daddy. And if you interfere with my plans, your wife will also learn about the cute, two-year-old another girlfriend of yours is raising up in New York."

"You asshole!" Robert swung at him.

With lightning speed, Malcolm ducked and delivered an uppercut. The force of the blow lifted the taller man off the floor. The second blow sailed across Robert's jaw, reeling him backward and sending his precious shades flying.

Robert quickly retaliated by throwing his weight into Malcolm.

Both men fell backward, into a glass table.

Neither heard the front door crash open.

"Break it up!" Jordan lifted Robert off his brother.

A loud crack resounded in the room when Robert's fist connected with Jordan's jaw.

Malcolm staggered to his feet, heedless of the

blood seeping from his shoulder, to come to his brother's aid.

Furniture crashed around them as the three men tumbled to the floor.

Alex was rounding the corner in the hallway when a deafening ruckus stole her attention. Seconds later she realized it was coming from her apartment. Apprehension and fear twisted inside her as she rushed to the open door.

Twenty-five

Nothing could have prepared Alex for what awaited her. In fact, it took a moment to comprehend what was happening.

"Stop it!" She rushed forward.

No one heard her.

She screamed again in vain, then thought of the self-protection alarm on her key ring. When she pressed the button, a loud shriek filled the room.

The men jumped apart and jerked their gazes toward her.

She released the button, satisfied she had their attention. "Look at what you've done to my apartment." She looked around.

Before the men spoke, neighbors crowded her open doorway, checking to see if everything was all right.

After the crowd had disbursed, her heated gaze narrowed on the three men. "I'm waiting."

Malcolm stood and helped his brother to his feet.

Robert remained on the floor, nursing his bruises.

"Alex, I'm sorry." Malcolm stepped forward. "It's my fault."

Jordan shook his head and assessed the room's destruction. "I'm so sorry, Alex. I didn't mean to get involved." He returned his attention to her. "Please let me help pay for the damages."

"I'll send you a bill." Her hands settled on her hips as she stared at Robert. "And what on earth are you doing here?"

He swiped the remaining shards of glass from his clothing. "I came here because we needed to talk. I didn't know that I'd be attacked." He glared at the brothers.

Tension blanketed the room while Malcolm suppressed the urge to strangle the jerk.

"I think I'd better go." Jordan volunteered, then glanced at his brother. "Maybe we can run that errand another time." As he headed toward the door, he apologized again, then slipped out.

She moved further into the room, dismayed at what she saw, and then returned her attention to her unwanted visitor. "I can't imagine we have anything further to say."

Malcolm took a protective stance behind her and wrapped an arm around her waist. To his surprise, she returned the gesture.

"Is there any way we can have this discussion without your so-called fiancé?" Robert said, sneering.

Alex's knees weakened as she glanced over her shoulder.

Tightening his hold to prevent her from falling, Malcolm waited for her to expose him.

She faced Robert. "There's nothing you can't say in front of Mal—my fiancé."

Malcolm loved the way the word sounded, and enjoyed the warmth it brought to his heart. His chin lifted as a wave of triumph washed over him.

Robert straightened his spine. "So it's true? You went off and got engaged?"

"I can't see how it's any of your business. You've made your decision." She pressed her fingers against her temples. "Look, I don't want to go through this again. It's all in the past. If you came here wanting to be involved in our child's life, we'll work something out. But if you came back wanting to be a part of my life, then that's impossible."

Malcolm sensed Robert's embarrassment, though he couldn't understand how a man could just walk away from an opportunity to be a part of his child's life.

Robert tilted his head. "If that's the way you want it." He walked toward the door and mumbled, "It probably isn't mine, anyway."

His callous remark knocked the wind out of her, but she allowed the matter to drop. The sooner he was out of her life, the better. But when the door slammed behind him, she wondered if she'd done the right thing. No matter what, a child had a right to know its father.

When Malcolm saw her troubled look, he encircled her in his embrace and placed a tender kiss against her forehead. "Don't worry. You did the right thing."

She gasped and pulled away. "You're bleeding."

He glanced at his shoulder, surprised at the amount of blood flowing from his wound. "It isn't as bad as it looks."

"Come on. Let's get you to the hospital." She pulled him forward.

He smiled, pleased by her concern. "I'm sure it's all right, sweetheart. Besides there's something I'm dying to show you."

"We shouldn't take chances. It could get infected."

He laughed, then pushed her toward the bedrooms. "After I show you something."

"It can wait—" Her eyes widened at the sight of the nursery. "I don't believe it."

"Do you like it?" He rubbed her shoulders as he stood behind her. "I did it myself." He pushed out his chest.

Alex jumped as she turned and wrapped her arms around him. "I love it!"

Malcolm howled in pain.

She jerked back. "Ohmigosh. I forgot about your shoulder. Will you please let me take you to a doctor now?"

"Might as well, before you kill me."

"I need to—especially after what you guys did to my living room."

"In that case, it would be worth it. I don't know what you ever saw in that guy, anyway." He shrugged. "He's really not that good-looking."

She smiled at his jealousy. "You know I kind of like the idea of you standing up for me. It's sort of like having my own knight in shining armor." She leaned over and kissed him tenderly. "Thanks."

He gazed down into her sultry eyes. "Don't mention it. That's what fiancés are for."

"I mean it, Noah." Rosa tapped her foot as she glared at him. "Things are going to change around here, starting right now." She turned and continued to throw away each liquor bottle from the bar.

He turned to leave the parlor.

"And where do you think you're going?"

He halted at her command. "Out!"

"Over my dead body," she said as she stormed toward him. "You're not leaving this house until this matter is settled."

"There's nothing to settle." His own anger mounted. He needed a drink, not his wife's constant flare of dramatics.

"The hell there isn't." She snatched a set of crumbled papers from the table. "Did you really think you were going to keep this from me?"

He averted his gaze, unable to face the disappointment in her eyes.

"These results practically say it's a miracle you're alive, and you're still standing there sulking because you can't have a damn drink. Are you crazy?" She threw the papers at him.

He said nothing when they hit his chest.

She shook her head at his continued silence. "Fine. If you want to kill yourself, I'm not going to stay here and watch."

She stalked past him, tears glistening in her eyes.

Noah's heart squeezed. "Where are you going?"

"I'm leaving you," she shouted without taking a backward glance, fearful that if she did she wouldn't go through with it.

He followed as words of desperation cluttered his mind. "Rosa—"

A loud thump drew her attention. She turned and gasped, seeing him sprawled across the floor. "Oh, dear God." She raced to his side.

He moaned as he tried to sit up.

"I'm going to call for help."

"No," he barked, shaking his head to clear it. "I'm all right. I just tripped, that's all."

She looked around, then shook her head in doubt. "Over what—air?"

"Please," he begged, his gaze locked with hers. "I'm fine. There's no reason to call anyone."

She hesitated. "Promise me you'll stop drinking."

He closed his eyes and agreed. "You won't tell anyone about what happened?"

She read fear in his eyes, and found herself nodding in compliance as tears finally crested her lashes and trickled down her face.

"Lucy, I'm home," Jordan called out in his best Ricky Ricardo voice. He thought nothing of it when Christian didn't answer. Either she hadn't made it home, or she hadn't heard him.

Stopping at the silver-framed mirror in the foyer, he checked to see if his jaw had swollen. He had to hand it to that guy. He packed quite a punch.

"Honey?" he called out, then performed a series of mouth stretches to ensure he hadn't broken anything.

For the first time, he noticed that the house seemed empty. He walked from the foyer to the parlor, then into the dining room.

The surprise of dinner not being ready had him mentally checking whether he'd forgotten something. He turned and raced back through the house and up the staircase, experiencing a strong sense of deja vu.

He burst through the bedroom door with his wife's name falling from his lips. He stopped and breathed a sigh of relief at the sight of Christian curled into a fetal position in the center of the bed.

Something was wrong.

"Chris—honey, are you all right?"

Her soft sobs were her only response.

His concern heightened as he touched her shoulder. "Sweetheart?"

Slowly, Christian uncurled her body and pulled up to prop against the pillows. Her bloodshot eyes said she'd been crying for a while.

"Come on, baby. Talk to me. What's wrong?"

"I . . . I don't know where to start." Her lips trembled.

With each tear that slid from her eyes, Jordan's heart tightened. "Please, don't do this to me. Tell me what's happened."

Her gaze met his and wavered. "I went to the doctor today. I don't know—I was experiencing some odd symptoms, but I didn't think it was anything serious."

Given her past medical history, he wasn't sure he wanted her to continue.

"I'm two months pregnant."

Silence.

He wasn't sure he'd heard her right. "Say that again."

"I know. I'm so happy." She hugged him and continued to sob in the curve of his neck.

"A baby?" His heart accelerated with hope, and his eyes instantly filled with tears. "Are you sure?"

She nodded, still unable to meet his eyes.

In one quick swoop, he lifted her from the bed and swung her around. "I don't believe it—a baby. We're going to have a baby!"

"Jordan, please put me down. I'm feeling nauseated."

"Oh, of course." He returned her to the bed. "Can I get you anything? Oh, wait until I tell Malcolm." His thoughts raced a mile a minute.

Christian started crying again.

Confused, he stated, "Honey, you don't look happy."

She sobbed louder.

"Or sound it." He pulled her back and gazed down at her. "Why all the tears?"

She started to talk, then shook her head.

Fear penetrated every fiber of his being as he waited patiently for her to speak.

"During the examination, the doctor detected a heart murmur. At first we thought that it might be something small, but he referred me to a cardiologist for an echocardiogram. Turns out I have a damaged valve."

"How was this not detected before?"

"I don't know." She sniffled.

"What does it mean?"

"Dr. McNally says that due to the stress of a pregnancy that somewhere around my sixth month I could suffer heart failure. Or if I try to go to full term, they fear I might need open heart surgery during delivery."

Jordan jerked back. "Are you saying that you could die if you go through with the pregnancy?"

Her tears fell in earnest again as her lips trembled violently, but her answer was clear. "Yes."

Twenty-six

"Hell, no," Jordan thundered, jumping from the bed. "It's out of the question."

Christian wiped at her tears and stood to face him. "What are you saying—that we terminate the pregnancy?"

"Yes . . . no." He shook his head as he stormed past her. "Hell, I don't know what I mean."

"Look, Jordan. I thought about this all afternoon, and I'm not sure about what to do, either." She dried her face.

His steps quickened as he paced the room, shaking his head. "I swear it seems like we're hit with one thing after another."

"I know," she said, deflated.

"What are we supposed to be deciding here— whether it's you or the baby?" His face twisted at the thought. He struggled to be logical, but logic couldn't possibly be applied to this situation.

"What we need to do is calm down and think this over rationally."

He stopped. "Have you already made a decision?" It was an accusation rather than a question, and when she looked away, he had his answer.

Her voice sounded strained as she spoke. "I want to have this baby."

He nodded bleakly, compressed his lips, and closed his eyes at the mere thought of losing her . . . again.

"It's the right thing to do." She stood in front of him. "It's what we always wanted."

"Says who?" He stepped back as if her touch burned. "My dreams always had you in them."

"This isn't a certainty. There's a chance that everything could go smoothly."

"I don't like the odds."

"I'm not crazy about them, either. But what choice do we have?" She blinked the tears from her lashes as she hugged herself. "Don't you want this baby?"

Desperately. He lowered his head, unable to speak.

"Say yes, damn it." Her whispered command quivered.

"Of course I want this—I want you, too. I'm sorry, but I *need* a guarantee that you'll survive."

"Well, I can't give it to you," she fairly screamed at him. "So now what?"

He felt cornered. What did he want? The way she glared at him made it nearly impossible to think. "Damn it, Christian. I don't know." He bolted to the door.

"Where are you going?"

"Out." He left the bedroom.

She followed him. "You have to be kidding."

"I need some air—I need a drink."

"What? Jordan, please—we need to finish talking about this."

"Oh, was that what we were doing? It felt more like an interrogation, if you ask me."

"You're not being fair. This isn't easy for me, either."

"It doesn't seem to me as if you need any help making decisions." He stopped at the edge of the staircase—twin urges to stay and leave assaulted him. When he looked back into her questioning gaze, he couldn't bear the weight of their world on his shoulders any longer. "What do you want from me? What do you want me to say?"

She exploded. "That I'm doing the right thing. I want to hear that you'll be here for me, supporting my decision."

He tossed up his hands in exasperation. "Fine. We'll do whatever *you* want to do, whatever *you* think is best." He stormed down the stairs. "Heaven knows you're always right about every damn thing, anyway."

The barb hurt. She lifted her chin and glared at him through a pool of tears. "Don't you dare walk out of this house."

"Why not? You sure as hell don't need me around here. You've made that quite obvious."

She raced behind him when he reached for

his jacket. "I mean it. We're not through talking."

"You may not be, but I am."

Christian jumped at the phone's sudden shrill tone.

Jordan snatched up the receiver from the small table in the foyer. "What?" he shouted.

"Thank God I found you," Charlotte said from the other end, her relief evident in her voice. "Have you seen the news?"

The abrupt change of subjects jarred Jordan's already muddled thoughts. "No, why?"

Christian crossed her arms and drummed her fingers impatiently.

"It's about Elliott, sir. He's dead."

"Dead?"

Christian straightened with instant concern.

"The police say it appears to be a suicide."

"That's not all," Charlotte continued. "He left a note—more like a catalogue of information. He's been sabotaging quite a lot of our projects, and even selling information to the highest bidder. One of the names mentioned is Michael Andrews."

"What? All of this is on the evening news?"

"Not all of it. My husband is one of the officers on the case, and I was able to get some information from him. But I'm sure the information is going to leak sooner or later."

"Are you at the office?"

"Where else?"

"I'll be down as soon as I can." He ended the call and his shoulders slumped forward.

"What is it? Who's dead?"

"Quentin Elliott. I swear, when it rains it pours. Seems like the man I just promoted was nothing more than a spy and a thief." He shook his head. "I don't know why I should be surprised. As the songs says—it weren't for bad luck . . ."

Panic coursed through her when his hand landed on the front doorknob. "When will you be back?"

"I don't know. Late."

"But—"

The door slammed behind him. She stared at it for several disbelieving seconds with her arms wrapped protectively around her body and her tears flowing freely down her face.

Noah listened intensely to the news with growing concern. What the tragedy meant to Jordan's company wasn't clear, but he could imagine the turmoil his son would be going through. An employee's betrayal often did more damage to an employer than to the company.

Images of the Compucom Systems president dominated most of the news coverage, but that didn't help much since he, too, was an ex-employee of Jordan's. What hurt Noah most was his inability to help.

As he sat and watched the news, Rosa's heartfelt pleas came flooding back. This wasn't the

first time he'd contemplated burying his pride,
but it was the first time the need consumed him.

In the morning, he'd agreed to check himself
into rehab. That was a big step in itself, and he
had a feeling he was about to make another.

He stood from his chair and headed toward
the door.

"I'm going to see him," he said at his wife's
inquisitive gaze as he passed.

Christian sat alone in the darkened parlor, patiently waiting for Jordan's return. Her tears had
long since dried. Numbness suppressed grief for
the moment, though she knew that would come,
too, as pain always followed a hard blow.

She didn't know what to do or what to say, and
she understood that her husband didn't know,
either. This was supposed to be a happy time in
their lives, and deep within her heart she embraced the miracle of the child she now carried,
but the possibility of what lay ahead scared her.

In vain, she tried to prepare a speech for her
husband's return, but no words seemed to be the
right ones. She rubbed her eyes—it felt as if
she'd been awake for an eternity. When she tried
to organize her thoughts, she only became frustrated with herself.

How many times had she sat in this very chair,
waiting for her husband's arrival? *Too many times
to count*, she answered in her mind, still unnerved
by the house's silence. The thought of actually

having the chance to fill these rooms with a child's laughter was a strong force in her decision.

As soon as Jordan allowed himself to calm down, she felt certain he'd come to the same conclusion, but surviving that wait—that threatened her sanity. She needed his support in this.

A pair of headlights drew her from her blue reverie, and she stood on shaky legs. Right now, she wanted nothing more than to put this whole thing behind them for the night and just lie in each other's arms.

She rushed to the door and opened it, prepared to do whatever she had to do to end the evening on a positive note. But when her eyes crashed with an older version of her husband, the sight momentarily jarred her.

"Noah?"

Twenty-seven

"Isn't this a switch?" Malcolm laughed as he glanced over his shoulder. "You bringing me home."

Alex's brow lifted inquisitively. "Careful, that sounds dangerously close to a sexist remark." She slid his key into the lock and opened it. When she switched on the light, she was more than amazed by the simple decor. She entered, glanced around, and nodded in approval. "Nice . . . and it's actually clean. You don't see that often with a bachelor."

"Now who's being sexist?"

She shrugged. "Two points for you."

His laughter died when a flicker of pain crossed his features. He pressed a hand to his bandaged shoulder.

"Are you all right?" She rushed to his side.

"Yeah, but it seems to hurt when I laugh."

"Then I would suggest you don't pass any mirrors."

"What are you trying to say?"

"That you look like a Mack truck hit you, then

backed up to finish the job." She turned and moved from the suite's entryway.

"You really have a way of cheering people up. I think you missed your true calling—to be a nurse."

She laughed, still turning on lights as she moved farther into the suite. "So how long have you lived here?"

"Just a few months. Can I get you something?"

"Nah. I still have to drive back home." She rechecked the items in the plastic bag she carried. "Here's everything we picked up from the pharmacy. Do I need to run out and get you anything else?"

"No, I think I have everything I need . . . well, just about." His gaze slid seductively over her body.

She laughed off the comment, but the room was suddenly charged with electricity. She swallowed, then licked her drying lips—a motion that brought a slow smile to Malcolm's handsome features.

"I should go." She hardly recognized her hoarse voice.

"I don't think that's a good idea." He moved closer, took the bag from her hands, and placed it on a nearby table. "I believe you want to stay."

You have no idea. "That would be a mistake." She forced her gaze lower, hoping to break his spell. There was no such luck. Her body paid no attention to the warnings her mind declared. Instead, she ached for his touch.

His fingers brushed against her cheek. "Our being together could never be a mistake."

Closing her eyes against the exotic images floating in her mind, she didn't dare trust herself to speak. And to her horror, tears seeped from her eyes. Her breath caught at the soft feel of his lips as they brushed against their tracks.

When he pulled away she opened her eyes, instantly mesmerized by his seductive gaze. Her heartbeat quickened. Words of protest were overruled by her heart. She'd wanted this—she wanted him.

"Stay with me tonight."

She couldn't respond.

His head descended and captured a kiss.

Her eyes drifted close as she savored him. His tongue invaded her mouth and danced a sweet duet with hers. Reality became a distant memory. All that mattered stood before her.

His lips deserted hers, but their taste lingered.

"Say you'll stay."

She licked her lips. "What about your shoulder?"

"Trust me. I can handle it, if you can."

A refusal sat on the tip of her tongue, but it was hard as hell to say.

"I know you want to," he added, without arrogance. "But I'll understand if you say no."

Her gaze returned to his dark penetrating one as a rejection crested her lips, but never reached her voice.

"Yes."

* * *

Jordan buried himself in paperwork and phone calls. He welcomed the work. The less time he spent obsessing over their dilemma the better.

Quentin's betrayal threatened to destroy J.W. Enterprises, and Jordan as well. How could he have done this to him? He forced the redundant question out of his mind. It was useless pondering over it. Nothing could change what had happened. The only thing left for him to do was to try to repair the damage.

"I knew I'd find you here."

Jordan froze at the familiar voice, then slowly lifted his gaze, momentarily startled to see his father standing in the doorway of his office. "What the hell are you doing here?"

"I could ask you the same question. I believe it's past your bedtime."

Jordan hung up the phone that had been perched on his shoulder. "Please don't tell me you came here to tuck me in—or maybe you came here to gloat?" He returned his attention to the piles of paper cluttering his desk, but not before he caught the wounded look on his father's face.

"Cheap shot," Noah finally replied, then moved farther into his son's office.

Jordan expelled a sigh of frustration as he leaned back in his chair, pinning his father with a hard stare. "All right, then, why *are* you here?"

He cringed at the sarcasm in his own voice, but damn if he could help the sudden anger.

"I came to help you.'"

"Help me?" His sarcasm sharpened. "Help me do what, exactly?"

"Jordan, I know you're angry."

"No. I'm not angry." His eyes narrowed. "I'm pissed." He jerked up from his chair. "For nearly fifteen years you have never once stepped foot in here, never offered to help. Where were you when I needed help getting started, or advice on how to run the damn place?" Jordan crashed his fist against the desk as he leaned forward. "And now, when your prediction of failure seems inevitable and I'm the top story on the evening news, I'm supposed to believe that you've suddenly turned into Saint Noah and come here to help?"

His father straightened. "I guess I deserve that." His voice quivered with raw emotion.

Guilt attacked Jordan in full force.

"And you're wrong. I've been here several times. Of course I never got farther than the front lobby." He lowered his gaze briefly. "Pride has cost me a lot over the years." Their eyes met again. "And I *did* help you get started, or rather I did what I could."

"What are you talking about?" An old suspicion resurfaced.

Noah cleared his throat. "Years ago, Mr. Lewis came to see me."

Jordan's jaw stiffened at the name of the NationsBank president.

"I think you know what I'm about to say."

Tension layered the room.

"So you're telling me I have you to thank for getting the loan on the building?"

"I was more than happy to help. I knew you would never ask."

Resentment burned in his chest. "Now why would I do that? Why would I give you the opportunity to gloat? No doubt you would have labeled me a failure."

Noah's handsome features crumbled. "I've said a lot of things I regret. I wish like hell I could take them back." He took a deep breath. "I know this comes a little late, but I'm sorry."

Jordan felt his stance slacken, not sure he could trust his ears. When his father moved to stand before his desk, he noticed the tired lines etched in his face and the pale-yellowish tint of his eyes.

Noah tried a different approach. "I was hurt, disappointed—"

Jordan's bitterness returned. "I know. You made *that* quite clear. Now, if this wonderful reunion is over, I have more important things on my mind."

"I need for you to know how very proud I am of all that you've accomplished. I'm very proud of both of my sons. A father can't ask for anything more than what you and Malcolm have given me, though I have a funny way of showing it."

Jordan crossed his arms and stared at him.

Noah continued. "I don't know what you expect me to say. Am I ashamed of what I allowed to happen? Yes. There isn't a single day that goes by that I don't regret what I've done, and my pride has been too great to rectify the problem. But I'm here now, and I pray that it's enough."

The tightening around Jordan's heart threatened to do him in, but he managed to hold his tongue and listen.

"I also came here to prevent you from making some of the same mistakes I've made."

Jordan's anger escaped in a long sigh.

Noah took his son's silence as encouragement to finish. "I know things are a little haywire around here right now. And I understand the need to get back on top of things. I truly do. But you need to go home to Christian. You have to save your marriage."

Jordan's shoulders shook with his sudden rumble of laughter. "Oh, this is priceless. You showed up here after all this time to give me marital advice?"

His father's expression remained somber. "I'm old and tired." He paused. "You know, up until this moment I couldn't admit that to myself. But I am. I'm very tired."

Jordan grew uncomfortable under his father's gaze.

"I've been where you're trying to get to. I've

run a successful company for over fifty years. I've let my job consume me, let it become my identity, and at times, sacrificed more than I should have. As far as marital advice goes, all I can tell you is—I miss all those vacations I never took. I miss every birthday, Valentine's Day, and anniversary when I wasn't there to tell your mother how much I loved her. How much I adored her."

"At least she's never threatened you with a divorce." Jordan surprised himself with the bitterness in his own voice.

"Don't I wish." Noah bristled. "In forty-three years of marriage I've managed to survive eight separations and two close call divorces."

Jordan's shock registered clearly on his face. "When? Why, what did you do?"

"Invested heavily in kneepads. I've done a lot of begging in my time." A sudden smile tugged at Noah's lips. "But the thing I regret most is that I allowed my ambitions for my company to sever my ties with you."

Jordan had a hard time grasping everything.

During the building silence, Noah drew in another deep breath. "I guess what I'm trying to say is that looking back, I've discovered that life's a bitch. And it's too easy to get caught up in the wrong things."

The men's gazes met again.

"Christian is a wonderful woman. I've enjoyed the many lunches and dinners she's sneaked off to have with me."

Jordan laughed unexpectedly. He wasn't surprised in the least. His wife had always been an active advocate for him to patch things up with his father. And now that the opportunity presented itself, he found that he was at a loss for words.

"I talked to her tonight, as well. She loves you," Noah continued. "And she needs you now more than ever." Guilt settled on his shoulders. "I'm sorry. Mostly for letting this go on for so long." He made sure he held his son's gaze. "I love you, and I'm so proud of the man you've become. But please, don't allow my past ideas of success cost you Christian's love. Go home."

Ashamed of the night's events, Jordan didn't toss out the possibility of his wife not being there. He'd said some mean things to her.

"Your work will never be able to give you what's waiting for you at home." Tears glossed Noah's eyes, but he held them at bay with weakening determination.

Fifteen years of animosity disappeared within the blink of an eye as Jordan opened his heart to reveal the truth. "I'm scared I'm going to lose her. In the past few months it's as if we've rediscovered ourselves, our love." His vision blurred, his tears threatening to win the war between them.

Jordan stood and paced the floor. "Before, I worked the long hours to prove to myself—and to you—that I could be a success. But I'm not in control. I don't give a damn about all of this." He pushed a pile of papers onto the floor.

"The company will survive. But I can't bear the thought of losing Christian—then, there's this miracle baby growing inside her, the child we've spent most of our lives dreaming about. How in the hell are we supposed to make this kind of decision?"

Noah stood before him. "I don't know, son. I'm not sure anyone does. But the right thing to do is to go to her and tell her how you feel."

"I know you're right." Jordan nodded. "Thank you for coming here tonight."

"I had to. It was long overdue." He opened his arms wide, and the two men embraced.

Twenty-eight

Malcolm's hands and mouth were like magic as they roamed over every inch of Alex's body. She arched against him as tears fell from her eyes. She had never felt so much love, nor given it so willingly in return.

She inhaled another shuddering breath and reflexively tightened her arms around him. "I missed you." Her voice was husky and low. He pulled her close and nuzzled kisses along the column of her neck.

When he cupped her full breasts, her breath caught in her throat, and her world spiraled out of control. Her eyes fluttered open. The room was still dark except for the moonlight spilling through the open curtains. She caught a glimpse of his handsome features through a mix of silvery light and black shadows.

Her fingers trembled as she slid them down the planes of his back. Aflame, her body begged for what was just beyond its reach.

Caught up in desire's fierce storm, her body

exploded with violent tremors as her nails clawed at his skin, and his name fell from her lips.

In the aftermath of their powerful lovemaking, she struggled to control her breathing. Her limbs were weak as drowsiness overtook her. She held no doubt that she'd need a week's worth of sleep to regain her strength.

Malcolm raised his head and gazed at her. "You could kill a man."

Mistaking his meaning, she shifted away from him. "I forgot about your shoulder," she said with wide-eyed concern.

"It's a little late to worry about that now, isn't it?" He laughed.

She blushed. "I'm sorry."

"Don't be," his voice lowered seductively. "Lord knows I'm not. In fact I think I'm about ready for round two."

"You're incorrigible."

"Lucky for you." He traced the outline of her lips with his fingers. "I thought this moment would never come," he confessed. His gaze centered on her. "When you left, I vowed that one day I would win you back. I just didn't think it would take so long."

Alex's eyes blurred as she remembered the day clearly. "That was one of the hardest things I've ever done."

Malcolm caressed her swollen abdomen. "I can't wait until our little boy arrives."

She smiled as she covered his hand. She caught his use of 'our' and experienced a rush of warmth throughout her body, but questions flooded her mind and erased her smile.

"I know that look." He eased up against the pillows, careful not to hurt his shoulder. "It means we're about to have a serious talk."

Her smile resurfaced. "You know me well."

"I consider it part of my job," he boasted, then sobered at her troubled look. "What's wrong, sweetheart?"

She slid comfortably beside him, not sure where to begin. "I guess I'm not sure what happens from here." She looked up into his smoldering gaze. "What do we truly want from each other?"

His smile remained tender as it widened. "I know exactly what I want—you."

She swallowed. There were no doubts about the sincerity of his words, and she reveled in the fact that his desire matched her own.

"But before you say anything," he added. "I want you to really think about how much time we've wasted trying to avoid just what happened between us. But if you ask me, this is exactly where we should be—together."

Tears crested her lashes as his head descended. His kiss was sweet and gentle. It, along with his heartfelt speech, had touched her heart. It was all true, she believed. They deserved to be together.

Jordan returned home with his weary emotions tangled into knots. It didn't surprise him that all the lights were off, but in the back of his head he tried to prepare for the possibility of his wife not being there.

"I'm glad to see you made it back."

At the sound of Christian's voice, he stilled his movements.

She switched on the light in the parlor.

At first sight of her tear-stained face, his heart broke. He walked over to her and instantly wrapped her pliant body in his arms. "I'm so sorry, baby."

She came unglued then, and her arms tightened around him. "When you left I felt so alone," she confessed.

"I'm here," he whispered, then kissed her furrowed brow. "I'll never leave you like that again. I promise." He led her over to the couch.

Once seated, he wiped away her tears—ashamed that he'd caused her so much pain. "Do you need me to get you anything?" he asked.

Christian shook her head—determined to gain control of her shattered emotions. "I'm all right."

He eased her back into his arms and expelled a worried sigh. "There's no excuse for some of the things I said to you earlier."

"Don't worry about it. It's okay."

"No, it's not. I took my anger out on you, when this entire situation is out of both of our hands."

She placed a silencing finger against his lips.

"Let's not talk about it any more tonight. I'm so tired of weighing the pros and cons, and conflicting emotions—I just don't think I'm up to it right now."

He nodded in understanding and continued to hold her as jasmine encircled his senses. He'd come to love the fragrance as much as he loved the woman.

Noah drove home feeling the best he had in years. His talk with Jordan had been long overdue, and it wasn't nearly as hard as he'd expected. He couldn't wait to share the news with Rosa.

Christian entered his mind. She held a sweet soul and was the perfect woman for his stubborn son, he thought. Smiling, he offered a quick prayer for a safe pregnancy.

As he turned onto his estate's long spiral driveway, he assessed and concluded he'd lived a good life. Stepping from the car, he hummed a tune he couldn't quite remember the name of and literally strolled to the door with pep in his step.

Everything was coming up roses. He thought about how much time Malcolm and Alexandria Cheney were spending together lately, and felt certain the two were destined to be together.

Entering the house, he glanced at his watch. Rosa must have retired for the night. Bypassing the opportunity to sneak a nightcap, he headed up the stairs two at a time. He went into the bedroom. As predicted, his wife was tucked beneath the sheets. Another smile lifted the corners of his lips, and he proceeded to dress for bed.

This time when he stopped in front of the mirror, he didn't mind the gray strands of hair, nor the fine lines in his face. Nothing could spoil his mood.

He slid under the sheets and eased his arm under Rosa. "I love you," he whispered. He kissed the back of her head and draped his other arm over her hip.

Before he drifted off to sleep, he heard her soft reply. "I love you, too."

As dawn approached, Noah, with a smile on his face and love flowing in his heart, drew his final breath.

Twenty-nine

Mourners packed the pews of Abernathy Baptist Church the Sunday following Noah's death. Special care went into every detail of the service. Colleagues, competitors, and age-old friends came to pay their respects.

The Williams family was grief-stricken.

Jordan was devastated as the weight of the world once again rested squarely on his shoulders. He doubted he could handle the pressure much longer, despite the strength he drew from Christian's touch.

He looked over at her and tried his best to give a reassuring smile, but the corners of his mouth only widened instead of curling upward. He squeezed her hand as Reverend Bowlin glided across the pulpit to begin the service.

Jordan lifted his head, careful to keep his gaze averted from the open casket. He struggled to focus on the service, but unwanted memories stole his concentration. The scene that remained most poignant in his mind was of their last talk together, and of his father's last words to him.

Noah's voice was crystal-clear in Jordan's mind. And he knew in his heart that despite everything he'd never stopped loving his father.

He rubbed Christian's hands while the backs of his eyes burned with unshed tears. The years they'd wasted did more than sicken him. The thought of them made him angry. But the bond that existed between father and son had never disappeared, and it wasn't until it was severed by Noah's death that Jordan truly felt its power.

No matter how mad he got with himself or with God, he and his father had been able to resolve their differences, and for that he was eternally grateful. Jordan closed his eyes and vowed to remain strong for his mother, if for no other reason.

Everything moved in slow motion as Rosa watched the funeral proceedings with a strange sense of detachment. Her pain had long since disappeared, and in its place emptiness existed. All that she was and all that she'd hoped to be lay inside the open casket before her.

Her black veil helped further separate her from the world of reality. In the week of Noah's passing, she hadn't shed a single tear—not even on the morning she'd discovered him lying so peacefully at her side. Instead, she'd caressed his face and whispered good-bye.

Malcolm and Jordan stood from the pews to give the eulogy. She saw the utter destruction sketched across their features, but she was unable to help them or console them, because she couldn't do it for herself.

At the end of the service, people milled around, offering condolences. They hugged her and their mouths moved, but she neither felt their embraces nor heard their words.

Her gaze was riveted to the casket. Noah's handsome face captured the perfect picture of serenity. The urge to curl up next to him nearly overpowered her. In fact, it seemed a natural thing to do. Here was a man she'd spent most her life loving and being loved by—and somewhere along the way they'd become one, which explained why when she looked at him, as she did now, she looked at herself.

Restless, she wanted everyone to leave her alone with her husband. An inner voice convinced her to continue to smile and thank everyone for coming, but she didn't know how much longer she could continue the charade.

Clarence brought up the end of the line.

The moment their gazes met, Rosa's façade cracked.

While he stood there, neither spoke. And yet, their silence spoke volumes. The backs of her eyes burned, and she suddenly became angry. She turned from the line and stormed away. She didn't want to feel anything. How dare he threaten her walls of security?

Jordan and Malcolm followed her.

"Momma, are you all right?" they asked in unison.

Rosa didn't hear them. She needed space. She needed air. Once outside the church she drew in a deep breath, and her knees instantly went weak.

Her sons caught her before she hit the ground.

"I've got her," Jordan claimed. "Go get some water. Maybe that will help revive her."

Without hesitation, Malcolm raced to do as his brother asked.

"Momma, are you all right?"

She lifted a trembling hand to her forehead as if to check for a fever.

"Say something," he urged nervously. When she still refused to speak, his anxieties heightened. He managed to suppress his own guilt and take charge. "I'm calling your doctor," he decided aloud.

Malcolm reappeared, with the water.

Jordan took the glass and literally forced her to take a sip.

"How is she?"

"I can't get her to say anything. Help me get her back inside, then I'll call her doctor."

"Maybe we should take her home. I don't think keeping her around here is going to help."

The hazy fog inside Rosa's head cleared somewhat when she heard the word home. They were going to make her leave. She couldn't leave Noah alone. Her strength returned and she struggled to stand on her own. "Let me go," she half shouted, half begged.

The brothers released her.

Her body trembled with defiance. "I'm fine now," she reassured with a butterfly smile. But from their expressions, she knew she hadn't convinced them. "Really. I just needed to get some air."

Jordan moved closer. "You could have hurt yourself had Malcolm and I not followed you out here. Perhaps you—"

"I said I was fine." She forced the issue with an air of desperation. Her body was suddenly accosted with a roller coaster of emotions she'd suppressed. "Please. I'm just not ready to leave."

Jordan hugged her. "I understand. We're not going to make you leave if you don't want to."

When his brother moved back, Malcolm embraced her and kissed the top of her head. "Do you want us to walk you back inside?"

Relief overwhelmed her as she nodded weakly. "I'd like that very much."

The men escorted her through the church door with their arms draped around her shoulders.

Christian stopped as she rounded the corner and saw the brothers reentering. She'd become concerned at Rosa's dramatic exit, but never having been her mother-in-law's favorite person, she'd thought it best to let Jordan follow her. But after so much time had passed, she decided to see if everything was all right.

When the women's gazes met, Christian waited for some scathing remark. Instead, she received an awkward smile. At first, she didn't know whether she should trust her eyes before she returned the gesture.

Rosa glanced to her sons. "Can you give us a few minutes?"

The request surprised everyone, and no one knew exactly what to say.

"Please," she added.

Jordan sought his wife's consent.

Christian nodded. When the men left them alone, she braided her hands before her.

"I want to thank you for coming," Rosa began, unsure herself why she felt compelled to talk to the woman she'd never welcomed into her family.

Christian took advantage of the silence to help ease the situation. "I needed and wanted to come. I don't know if you were aware of it, but I spoke with Noah quite a bit over the years. He was a great man."

"Yes, he was." Rosa looked away. It pained her to talk of him in the past tense. Once again those crazed emotions came to the surface. "But he could be stubborn." When she thought of his drinking, betrayal squeezed her heart. "I guess that made us two peas in a pod." Her gaze returned to her daughter-in-law. "I owe you a big apology."

Christian's breath caught in her throat. She'd dreamed of this moment for years, and now that it had presented itself, it seemed surreal. "I don't think that's necessary."

"It's way overdue. I've spent years blaming you

for the estrangement between Noah and Jordan. But deep down I always knew it wasn't true. Pride has cost this family a great deal. I know that now. It cost Noah a son, and it's robbed me of a daughter."

Christian stepped forward, then suddenly unsure of herself, stopped.

Rosa closed the distance. "Can you find it in your heart to ever forgive me?"

"I already have. I would like it so very much for us to become friends."

"I would rather we became a family."

For the first time, the two women embraced, erasing over a decade of pain and heartache.

That evening, Malcolm and Alex drove home in silence. Malcolm wanted to continue driving forever. Nothing would ever be the same again. He hated the way he felt, but he welcomed the pain that throbbed in his soul. It was a reminder that he was still among the living because a part of him had died with his hero.

He fought the rage building inside of him with as much vehemence as he did his anguish. Why hadn't he seen what was coming? All the signs were there. Maybe he just hadn't wanted to see them.

Alex caressed his cheek.

He turned slightly into her touch, relishing more than just her presence. She had made the past week bearable. The next road he turned down brought her apartment building into view. He wasn't ready for her to leave him—not yet.

"Are you going to be all right tonight?" Concern layered her voice.

He glanced over at her, and swore he was staring into the face of love. He returned his attention to the road. "Yeah, I'll be fine."

"I'm worried about you." Her hand moved to thread through the short strands of his hair. "Why don't you stay at my place tonight?"

Malcolm's heart warmed. He'd like nothing more than to spend the night curled in her arms, holding his hope for the future. Her hand settled on his shoulders, soliciting another glance in her direction.

"I want you to stay," she added.

There was no way on God's green earth he was going to turn her down. And she knew it.

When they entered her apartment, Malcolm felt as if he were returning home. Strange, he thought, of how they'd slid into a relationship without either of them admitting what it was. It was as if they had both been testing the waters before diving in.

Alex fixed him a nightcap, then prepared a cup of warm milk for herself before settling on the sofa.

He looked at the amber liquid and had no desire to drink it. Noah died from cirrhosis of the liver. His favorite pastime had finally caught up with him. Pushing the drink aside, Malcolm decided to quit.

Alex nestled in the curve of his arm and laid her head against his chest.

"I love you," she whispered.

Jerked from his reverie, he wasn't quite sure he'd heard her correctly.

She sat up and met his inquisitive gaze. "I do. And probably more than you'll ever know."

"I more than love you," he replied. "I'm *in* love with you."

"Then what are we going to do about it?"

Her directness surprised him, but he knew from the look in her eyes that they were engaged in the most important conversation of their lives.

"If I had my way, we would spend the rest of our lives making up for lost time," he answered seriously. "I've been honest with you about how I feel. I loved you yesterday, I love you today, and I'll love you tomorrow." He reached out and brushed his fingers against her cheek. "You'll never know how many times I stared up at the stars wondering where you were or what you were doing, and wishing like hell I could be there with you."

She took his hand and kissed it.

"Mind if I ask what brought all this up?"

Alex hesitated, then answered with an awkward smile. "Your father." She looked up and eased closer at the heart-wrenching pain streaked across his face. "What I mean is—I keep thinking about him and Jordan, and even you and me. Look at how much time we all lost. Time we can never get back. It's almost sad how we all take each other for granted. In my mind, I've always known you were out there, probably loving me as much as I did you. We were apart, but not really." She shook her head at how crazy that sounded.

Malcolm lowered his gaze and contemplated asking the question that dominated his thoughts. "What about Robert?"

She drew a deep breath wondering where to begin. "At one time I did care for him. I overlooked the obvious signs of his infidelity, and ignored the inconsistency of his stories. I think I was in a relationship just to be in one. But I never loved him."

She stood from the sofa, suddenly uneasy about her confession. "That was probably a terrible thing to say about a man whose child I'm carrying."

Malcolm stood as relief flooded every pore of his body. He pulled her close and tilted her head so their gazes could meet. "I'd be lying if I said I wasn't jealous. But at the same time, I can't wait for the little rugrat to get here."

He smiled at her puzzled look before he continued. "Alex, this child is also a part of you. How could I not love it?"

The sincerity of his words lingered in his eyes and her heart melted.

"Marry me," he said.

Thirty

Jordan stared up into the bedroom's darkness without much hope of getting any sleep. The day's events replayed in his mind, and deepened his depression.

In retrospect, the time wasted over something so trivial sickened him. But no matter what he did, nothing could change the past, and nothing could bring his father back. There was a lesson to be learned about all of this. He tightened his embrace.

Christian snuggled closer.

Nothing was more important than family. He just wished he'd learned the lesson sooner. He shifted his attention to his wife as she lay peacefully in his arms. The possibility of losing her after all they'd been through seemed incomprehensible. But he was at God's mercy.

He rested his free hand against her stomach and thought of all the possibilities that lay ahead. Yes, now more than ever, he wanted this child. But, as his eyes drifted to Christian's beautiful face, he wasn't prepared to face what their desire might cost them.

Staring at her serene features, the desire to make love to her strengthened. Yet, he refused to do anything that would jeopardize her and the pregnancy, so he remained content with just holding her and enjoying the fresh scent of jasmine.

Rosa flipped through numerous family albums, hoping to recapture the joy of days gone by. She succeeded with some, but failed with others. When she came across her wedding pictures, she stopped.

Noah's youthful and handsome face smiled at a younger image of herself. It was the happiest day of her life.

She stumbled across Jordan and Malcolm's first baby pictures and smiled warmly at her two bundles of joy. As she turned the pages, years passed in a matter of minutes. And soon, tears trickled from her eyes.

She had no right to complain about anything. She'd had a terrific husband, great children, and a wonderful life.

However, her albums were missing pictures of Jordan's wedding. Shame washed over her in waves. For years she'd badgered Noah and Jordan to resolve their differences when all along she was the hypocrite.

Now, Jordan and Christian were expecting

their first child. And Christian's life was in danger. Rosa hoped she'd taken the first step in bridging the gap.

She closed the albums. She would miss her husband every day of her life, yet she needed to look to the future and embrace her family. And Christian was a part of that family. From that day forth she vowed she would make sure her daughter-in-law knew just that.

Christian opened her eyes, but made no effort to get out of bed. Instead, she turned to the vacant spot beside her and frowned.

The bedroom's door swung open and Jordan entered carrying a tray loaded with food. "I thought you might enjoy breakfast in bed." His brows wriggled playfully as he walked toward her.

"You cooked?" She propped up against the pillows.

"Well, Clarence coached," he replied shyly before sharing a tender kiss. "How are we feeling this morning?"

She drew in a deep breath as she thought for a moment. Today was the last safe day to terminate the pregnancy, but they'd decided against it. "Nervous." She exhaled.

He eased over to his side of the bed. "That makes two of us."

An awkward silence entombed them.

Christian bit into a plump strawberry and tried to think of a way to broach the subject.

"You still want to go through with this, don't you?"

Unable to determine his mood by the tone of his voice, she opened her mouth to answer, but no words came. She nodded instead.

Jordan expelled a long sigh.

"I wish you could just understand." She looked up at him.

"I do. But I wish I didn't. It would make things a hell of a lot easier. So much has happened in the last few months. There are a lot of things I regret, but at the same time, I've learned a great deal." He edged closer.

Christian removed the tray and set it beside the bed.

Jordan pulled his wife into his arms. "My company will bounce back, Malcolm is fully capable of running Opulence, and my mother is a strong woman. I know she'll get through this. And I plan to be there for her every step of the way. As for Noah, he'll always be right here." He covered his heart with his hand. There's comfort in knowing that." Tears pooled in his eyes. "But I pray I'll always have you by my side."

Christian heard the fear in his voice for what it was. "Please say you're with me on this." Hope flared and echoed in her voice.

Jordan reached up and caressed her face. "Will you never realize how much I love you?" He watched as her eyes glossed over. "Of course I'm with you on this. We're in this together."

"I love you." She kissed him.

When he pulled back and gazed down at her, he knew he'd made the right decision. And he'd promised himself he wouldn't mull over the risks of carrying the baby to term. "I'm in love with you. And we're going to have a baby." A tear streaked down his face as he closed his eyes and prayed that he'd always be surrounded by jasmine.

Epilogue

One year later

Rain clouds dominated the sky and threatened to ruin Jordan's visit to Hillandale Memorial Cemetery. Steady winds rustled the grass and flowers around the lone grave. In the air, the soft scent of jasmine lingered.

Jordan stood above the grave, struggling for the right words—the perfect turn of phrase—that would express what was in his heart.

"There's not a day that goes by that I don't miss you, or miss all the things we'll never do as a family." His voice quivered.

After all this time, the visits weren't getting any easier—they were harder. He drew in a shaky breath and prayed for strength. "I wish you could see our baby girl. We've started calling her little Bobby. I can't tell you how much the family at McKinley Ranch loves that." He laughed, but the sound was awkward to his own ears. "She's really smart. I have no doubt I'll have my hands full fighting off the boys one day." He shook his head. "I'm not looking forward to that."

Remembering the flowers he held in his hands, he leaned down and carefully placed them in front of the tombstone. He couldn't resist the urge to run his fingers along the name. "When I think about you, I . . ."

He pressed his lips together, unable to finish his sentence. He looked around the beautifully manicured lawn with a pang of regret and remorse. "Mom's doing well. She just adores little Bobby. And I know you won't believe this, but Alex and Malcolm are expecting again. Their first son, Drake, is an exact replica of his mother., He's a good boy." Jordan's vision blurred.

An arm slid around his waist, and he turned as Christian leaned over to offer a kiss of encouragement. On her hip, she carried five-month-old Bobby, while little Noah still sat in the twin stroller.

He smiled, then returned his attention to his father's grave. "As I was saying, Pop—Malcolm and Alex are doing well. I figured you should know that. Especially since I don't know the next time Mal can make it up here. I'm sure he's jumping through hoops. I should know—the twins keep us pretty busy.

He fell silent.

Christian moved closer. "Are you all right, sweetheart?"

He nodded, and once again thanked God that

he hadn't lost her as well. In fact, there wasn't a day that went by that he wasn't grateful for her still being by his side. He retrieved Noah from the stroller, then turned and embraced his small family, perhaps squeezing them harder than usual. "I love you," he whispered.

She clung to her husband, then withdrew to gaze into his eyes. "I love you, too."

"Laa, da da," Bobby shouted, clapping her small hands together.

Her parents laughed and kissed her chubby cheeks. "We laa you, too, sweetie."

A NOTE FROM THE AUTHOR

It's so hard to say good-bye to friends. Which is how I feel for Christian, Jordan, Malcolm and Alex. I think it's because for me these characters inspire hope and prove that love truly conquers all. I also want to take the time to thank you for the overwhelming response to I PROMISE. Those who shared with me their own stories of dealing with breast cancer touched me.

Again, I want to stress the importance of early detection. According to the American Cancer Society, among women younger than fifty years of age, African-American women are most likely to develop breast cancer. Please feel free to contact ACS toll free: 800-ACS-2345.

May God bless you and inspire you to love.

Adrianne

Adrianne Byrd
6540-C Hillandale Dr.
Norcross, GA 30092
Abryd2000@aol.com

About the Author

Adrian Byrd resides between her homes in Memphis, TN, Sunnyvale, CA and Marietta, GA. This former entertainer has loved romance novels half her life and started writing professionally before finishing high school. Her goals are to continue to write novels and start a budding career in screenwriting.

Coming in February from
Arabesque Books . . .

TENDER ESCAPE by Candice Poarch
1-58314-082-4 $5.99US/$7.99CAN

After Olivia Hammond's husband is killed, rumors surface that he was a criminal and she must work with investigator Clifton Zayne in order to solve the mystery. Soon, a passion between the two is ignited which just may begin to heal the old wounds of love gone by . . .

A FOREVER PASSION by Angela Winters
1-58314-077-8 $5.99US/$7.99CAN

When congressman Marcus Hart hires Sydney Tanner for a genealogy research project on his family, he is instantly intrigued with her cool attitude. But they must confront unbelievable family resistance and simmering, long-kept secrets together if they are to gain a world of love.

REAL LOVE by Marcella Sanders
1-58314-075-1 $5.99US/$7.99CAN

When longtime friends Monique McRay and Nick Parker enter into a sham marriage so that Nick can inherit land for a children's camp, neither of them expect the undeniable sensual heat building between them—just as neither of them can resist when their passion is finally ignited.

CUPID'S ARROW
by Layle Giusto, Doris Johnson, and Jacquelin Thomas
1-58314-076-X $5.99US/$7.99CAN

It's the moment that catches your breath and sends your world reeling; when you know your life will never be the same. It's the moment when you fall passionately, hopelessly in love. Experience that breathtaking feeling with these unforgettable Valentine's Day tales . . .

__Please Use the Coupon on the Next Page to Order__

Celebrate Valentine's Day with Arabesque Books

__TENDER ESCAPE__ by Candice Poarch
     1-58314-082-4 $5.99US/$7.99CAN

__A FOREVER PASSION__ by Angela Winters
     1-58314-077-8 $5.99US/$7.99CAN

__REAL LOVE__ by Marcella Sanders
     1-58314-075-1 $5.99US/$7.99CAN

__CUPID'S ARROW__
by Layle Giusto, Doris Johnson, and Jacquelin Thomas
     1-58314-076-X $5.99US/$7.99CAN

THESE ARABESQUE ROMANCES
ARE NOW MOVIES FROM BET!

SIZZLING ROMANCE BY *ROCHELLE ALERS*

SUMMER MAGIC   1-58314-012-3 $4.99US/$6.50CAN
When Caryn Edwards rented a summer house in North Carolina, she never knew she'd have to share it with handsome developer Logan Prescott. Soon, their mutual distrust dissolves and passion takes over—but can the magic last when the autumn comes?

HAPPILY EVER AFTER   0-7860-0064-3 $4.99US/$6.50CAN
Lauren Taylor's heartbreaking divorce has left her with little more than memories of sensuous tropical nights and long-gone happiness. Now her ex is back in Boston with an offer she can't refuse and a chance to start over with a man she'd lost once before.

HEAVEN SENT   0-7860-0530-0 $4.99US/$6.50CAN
When Serena Morris-Vega visits Costa Rica, she finds herself saving an ailing corporate CEO's life. In the process, she discovers secrets about his true identity . . . and an all-consuming passion for this mysterious stranger.

HIDDEN AGENDA   0-7860-0041-4 $4.99US/$6.50CAN
After Eve Blackwell hires the dangerous and irresistable Matt Sterling to find her abducted son, she must enter into a charade of marriage with him on a journey from Virginia to Mexico . . . but their attraction is too strong to remain a charade for long.

HIDEAWAY   0-7860-0135-6 $4.99US/$6.50CAN
Parris Simmons has spent the last ten years hiding from her past. But when her ex-lover finds her and offers her the protection of his name, she agrees to marry him and their desire reignites—until a dangerous secret threatens to destroy everything they cherish most.

HOME SWEET HOME   0-7860-0276-X $4.99US/$6.50CAN
When Quintin Lord meets his new neighbor, ballerina-turned-caterer Victoria Jones, he is surprised and enchanted by her grace. But love has cost her and she will not put her heart on the line again—until Quintin proves to her that a lasting love is worth any risk.

VOWS   0-7860-0463-0 $4.99US/$6.50CAN
After practical accountant Vanessa Blanchard is seduced by Joshua Kirkland while on vacation, she is left with unanswered questions and sleepless nights of remembered ecstasy. For Joshua, his game of seduction has become a daring race to protect the woman he loves . . .

USE COUPON ON NEXT PAGE TO ORDER THESE BOOKS